CHARLIE HOOPER, DETECTIVE:

CHARLIE HOOPER, DETECTIVE:

THE CASE OF THE SCHOOL PHANTOMS

A Pinesdale Sleuths Mystery
Book 1

Carol A. Lanier

Illustrated by D.G. Henderson

WestBow
PRESS

Copyright © 2012 Carol A. Lanier

All rights reserved. No part of this book may be used or reproduced by any means, graphic, electronic, or mechanical, including photocopying, recording, taping or by any information storage retrieval system without the written permission of the publisher except in the case of brief quotations embodied in critical articles and reviews.

Names and places, except for Civil War, used in this work are fictional.
Any similarity to actual names and places is coincidental.
Bible quotations are from the New International Version unless otherwise noted.

WestBow Press books may be ordered through booksellers or by contacting:

WestBow Press
A Division of Thomas Nelson
1663 Liberty Drive
Bloomington, IN 47403
www.westbowpress.com
1-(866) 928-1240

Because of the dynamic nature of the Internet, any web addresses or links contained in this book may have changed since publication and may no longer be valid. The views expressed in this work are solely those of the author and do not necessarily reflect the views of the publisher, and the publisher hereby disclaims any responsibility for them.

Any people depicted in stock imagery provided by Thinkstock are models, and such images are being used for illustrative purposes only.

Certain stock imagery © Thinkstock.

ISBN: 978-1-4497-4106-8 (sc)
ISBN: 978-1-4497-4107-5 (hc)
ISBN: 978-1-4497-4105-1 (e)
Library of Congress Control Number: 2012903213

Printed in the United States of America

WestBow Press rev. date: 5/2/2012

Dedication

To God, for his honor and glory, and to all young people who love to read.

A friend loves at all times.
Proverbs 17:17a, NIV

Contents

Prologue xi
Chapter 1. The Summer Ends 1
Chapter 2. The Phantom? 9
Chapter 3. The Flashback 21
Chapter 4. A Mysterious Clue 33
Chapter 5. The Haunted Mansion 45
Chapter 6. Nosy Nate 57
Chapter 7. Another Heist 69
Chapter 8. More Puzzling Clues 83
Chapter 9. In Disguise 95
Chapter 10. The Secret Room 105
Chapter 11. Trapped! 115
Chapter 12. Trouble at the Gazebo 129
Chapter 13. The Hidden Cabin 139
Chapter 14. The Chase 145
Chapter 15. Cooked Crooks! 153

List of Illustrations

1. Door of Crime Scene—Chapter 2
2. Folded Note—Chapter 4
3. Sleuths in Treehouse—Chapter 4
4. The Mason Mansion—Chapter 5
5. Break-in at School—Chapter 7
6. Nancy Kidnapped—Chapter 7
7. Charlie Under the Pier—Chapter 8
8. The Ballroom—Chapter 10
9. The Attic Key—Chapter 11
10. The Gazebo—Chapter 12
11. Charlie Tackles Nate—Chapter 15

Many thanks to Wanda Burquest, a true friend and dedicated writing assistant, who always goes the extra mile; to DeAnne Henderson for her creativity and willingness to help this perfect stranger with illustrations; to the Heart of Georgia Writers Group (HOG) for their suggestions and encouragement; to Grayson Gould (age eight) and Abby Hammack (age 13), for graciously reading the early manuscript and giving their approval; to Alissa Peacock, my first helper; to my family and friends for their support.

Prologue

July

Charlie Hooper sat on a round braided rug in his treehouse, munching on a pimento cheese sandwich and a juicy apple. He smiled, remembering building the rugged treehouse with his dad and grandpa a few years before. He'd almost tumbled out when they lowered the ladder, but his dad grabbed him by the belt just in time, and Grandpa smashed his thumb when nailing boards.

His spine tingled as he thought about investigating mysteries like his grandpa did. He smiled again. *Solving the mystery of the missing necklace was awesome, but I hope my friends and I solve another one.*

Dear Lord, thank you for my grandpa. He is the best detective Pinesdale has ever known. Help me be like him, wise and kind and a great detective.

Bam! Charlie heard the back door slam. He jumped up, yelling as he ran. "Hey, Dad, Grandpa's home!" He slammed into his grandfather, giving him a big hug. He stepped back. "What's up? You look like something's wrong."

"Charlie, I have some bad news. I had to arrest Earl Thatcher for drug dealing today. I know you and Nate are friends at school."

"What will happen to Nate?" Charlie asked. "Dad, will you represent his father? You're a great attorney."

"Mr. Thatcher has his own lawyer, son." Dad rumpled Charlie's hair. "It's nice of you to be concerned about your friend's father."

"The Social Services Department is planning to place Nate with his uncle, his only living relative," Grandpa answered.

"He's not very nice, is he?"

"We'll have to hope for the best and pray for Nate." Grandpa looked serious. "What's happened has turned his world upside-down, and he could sure use a friend."

Charlie knew some kids would reject Nate, because of his dad's arrest. "I'll stick by him, Grandpa."

"That's our Lord's way," Grandpa said. "Sticking closer than a brother."

A few days later

Br-r-r-ing! The phone rang as Charlie ran through the front door.

"Hello?" his mom answered. "Oh, no!" Her face turned white as she slowly sank into a chair. "We'll be right there." Tears came to her eyes. The phone slipped from her hand.

"Mom, what's the matter?" Charlie yelled in a frantic tone. "Are you okay?"

Trembling, she pulled him close to her. "Something terrible has happened. Your dad and grandfather have been in a car accident. We've got to hurry to the hospital."

Charlie sat in a waiting room chair with his head in his hands, blinking back the tears. *God, please let them be all right.*

His mom was talking to the doctor. The doctor shook his head. "I'm sorry. We did everything possible, but we couldn't save them."

Charlie rushed to her, squeezing his arms around her waist.

"We'll be okay," she assured him with a strong voice. "God will take care of us."

That afternoon, the doorbell rang. Charlie opened the door to Pastor Burns.

"Hi, Charlie, is your mom home?"

"Mom, the preacher's here to see you."

His mom came from the kitchen. "Pastor, thank you for coming."

"I heard about the accident. I wanted to say how sorry I am and to see if there's anything I can do. Is this a good time to go over the details of the funeral service?"

"Yes, that would be helpful. Chief Howard hasn't been by yet. Do you know what caused the crash?" she asked, wiping tears with her handkerchief.

"I heard a boy on his bike pulled out in front of the car. Mike swerved to miss him, losing control. He went into the other lane. A tractor-trailer truck hit them broadside."

"Oh, no!" she murmured. "What was a boy doing out on the highway?" She wiped more tears. "Is he okay?"

"Only scratches and bruises. I understand he knows Charlie."

"Who is it?" Charlie clutched his mom's hand.

"His name is Nate Thatcher."

Charlie's face flushed and he fled to his room. He flung himself on his bed and cried.

A week later, Charlie bumped into Nate at Floyd's Grocery Store. He reached out his hand to touch Nate's shoulder. "Sorry about your dad going to prison. And I know the car crash was an accident. We can still be friends, right?"

Nate slung Charlie's hand off. "Get out of my way and leave me alone! I don't need you or want you around anymore. I have other friends to hang out with now!" He stalked away, mad as a snorting bull.

God, Charlie prayed, *help me not to be upset with Nate. I'm supposed to always be a friend. But how can I, when he doesn't want anything to do with me?*

Chapter 1
THE SUMMER ENDS

August

Charlie sped down his quiet street, Courtwood Drive, popping a wheelie on his new sporty bike. Big oak trees stood in each yard. *I'll have a lot of raking to do this winter, he thought.* The hot breeze tousled his wavy brown hair while he waited for his best friends to go to the park. Rick and Rae Casson were twins who had lived next door since second grade. They had just returned from summer camp. He stopped when he saw them push their bikes out of their garage.

"Hey, y'all," he called, "how was camp? I missed you like crazy!"

"It's great to be home," Rick said, pulling up in front of him. "I really missed this small town of ours."

"Camp was fun, but we missed you, too." Rae stopped. She put a ball cap over her short blond hair. "Rick and I were sorry to hear about your dad and grandpa."

"Yeah," Rick added. "Wish we'd been here for you."

"Thanks. I miss them so much." Charlie turned his bike around. "Race you to the park!"

In a couple of minutes, they put their bikes in the rack. "Did you solve any more mysteries while we were gone?" Rick asked.

Charlie sighed. "No, but I'm hoping we will soon."

"I heard seventh grade is tough," Rick said. "I wonder who our teachers will be."

"I don't care, as long as Nate Thatcher isn't there!" Charlie said in an irritated tone.

"You sure don't like him anymore, do you?" Rae asked.

"Why should I? Since his dad went to prison and the accident, he's become a pest and always causes trouble."

At that moment, they heard shouts from across the park.

"What's that?" Rick asked.

The friends hurried across and found Nate scuffling with a sixth grader. Nate threw him to the ground. "You little snitch!" he snarled, gritting his teeth. "Why did you tell on me? Mr. Taylor said if I stole any more candy from his store, he'd call the police."

"I won't snitch again," the younger boy cried.

Nate slapped him on the back of his head. "Make sure you don't," he yelled.

"Can I help?" Charlie asked the boy, reaching down to pull him up.

"I'm okay," he said. Trembling, he ran to join his friends.

Charlie turned to Nate. "Do you always have to be such a bully? I know why you pick on smaller kids. You're mad at everyone."

Nate poked his fist in Charlie's face, jabbing him in the jaw. "You're a coward and you'll never be like your grandfather!" He turned on his heel and stomped away.

"That Nate Thatcher is as mean as a rattlesnake," Rae said. "I guess it's because he repeated first grade and has home problems."

"Yeah, let's forget about Nate." Charlie rubbed his sore jaw. "I'm starving!"

As he and the twins headed home, Charlie couldn't get Nate's hurtful words out of his mind. *I suppose Nate is having a really hard time with his dad in prison. Maybe that's why he acts the way he does. But he sure makes me mad. God, help me be his friend.*

Rounding a corner, he caught a glimpse of the old Mason Mansion. He put on his brake. "Hold up a second. Why don't we explore the mansion? I've never been inside. It looks mysterious."

Rae looked at him with narrowed eyes. "Thought you were starvin', Charlie."

He pedaled closer to the mansion. "Food can wait when there might be a mystery!" he called back over his shoulder.

"That's a first!" she muttered under her breath.

"It's a spooky-looking place," Rick replied, following Charlie.

"And really run-down," Rae added, pulling up alongside the boys. "Do you think it's haunted?"

"I never heard that it's haunted. There's no such thing as ghosts anyway." Charlie turned to look at the mansion. "My grandmother said it used to be a beautiful place and was open for tours. Let's take a peek through the space in that window. We're not scared, are we?"

Rae shivered. "Oh, it looks dusty, dirty *and* scary to me. Why don't they keep it clean and give tours?"

"I think they ran out of money to keep it up."

"Has anybody gone in it lately?" Rick asked.

"I doubt it, but there's no sign saying we can't," Charlie said.

Bang! A door suddenly slammed inside the mansion.

"What was that? Is someone in there? It must be h-h-h-au-nted!" Rae stammered.

"Don't be silly. I told you, there's no such thing. How about checking it out?" Charlie encouraged them. "The bang was probably the wind. Come on."

Charlie stepped on the porch of the shabby mansion. The brick wall looked faded and worn. His quivering hand clutched the doorknob of the tall front door. He pushed it open with both hands and entered the hall. Charlie stopped in a cold sweat. *The place does look creepy,* he thought. "Come on, you two. Maybe we'll find a mystery in here."

Rick and Rae rushed inside, tumbling into Charlie. The three tiptoed to the back of the large entry hall. They opened a door and stepped into a big kitchen. A small door in the wall slowly closed with a sharp click. Charlie tried tugging at the handle, but the door wouldn't open. They looked at each other in fear.

Rae shook with fright. "No ghosts, huh?"

Charlie couldn't believe his eyes, but knew there had to be an explanation. *Who's behind the door?*

"Maybe it's Nate trying to frighten us," Rick said.

"You could be right," Charlie agreed.

Rae pulled at Charlie's arm. "I'm scared. Let's get out of here."

The friends scrambled toward the front entrance.

"Whoa!" Charlie called, glancing into the room to the right of the foyer. "Look at this. Someone broke a vase."

"It looks expensive." Rae poked a finger at the pieces. "It's not covered in dust like everything else. Must've happened not long ago."

"You're right," Charlie said. "There *is* a mystery here! Who could've done this?" Goosebumps popped out on his arms. "Let's get out of here!"

As he jumped on his bike, a noise startled him. The leaves from the large oak trees surrounding the old house rustled. Someone darted from behind the mansion.

Was it Nate?

Chapter 2

THE PHANTOM?

"Hey, Charlie, what's up?" a friend called. Others waved to him. He smiled, lifted his chin, and waved back. On the first day of school, he strolled down the light-green hall of Pinesdale Middle School. It smelled of fresh paint and floor wax. Crowds of talkative students moved steadily toward the school cafeteria where they would pick up their class schedules and locker assignments.

Rick slung his arm around Charlie's shoulder. "How're things goin', friend? Ready to tackle seventh grade?"

"It may not be as tough as we heard," Rae said. She bumped into a dark-haired girl. "Oops! Sorry."

"Oh, it's okay," the girl said. "I'm totally turned around. Can you tell me where the cafeteria is?"

Rae smiled. "Sure, walk with us. We're going that way. You must be new. What's your name? What grade are you in?"

"I'm in seventh grade and I *am* new. My name is Nancy. What's yours?"

"I'm Rae. This is Rick and Charlie. Welcome to Pinesdale Middle School. Let me know if I can help you find your way around. I'm sure we'll have some classes together."

"Yeah, we're all in seventh grade," Charlie said. "We'd better get going so we can get our locker numbers and schedules."

Arriving at the cafeteria, he spotted the table labeled "H-J." He reached out to take his number. His mouth gaped open. "Locker #13! I'm doomed!" he gasped, staring at the paper in horror.

"Yeah," Rick said. "Everybody knows about number thirteen—the worst one in the school! It's almost impossible to get open. Hope the other kids don't hassle you too much." He motioned to his twin sister. "Come on, Rae. We'd better get to our lockers."

Charlie kept fidgeting with the combination lock. *Click!* "Finally!" he mumbled, jerking open the door.

He gripped his books and slammed the locker shut. When he rounded the corner, Nate Thatcher crashed into him. Books flew everywhere. Then the bell rang.

"You clumsy ox!" Charlie yelled. "Now I'll be late for sure!"

"Aw, don't get out of joint. Your teacher won't kill you." Nate snatched a book from Charlie's hands. "You think you're the teacher's pet, but you're a loser."

"Give me my book, Nate. You're a bully and a show-off. I tried to be a friend, but you won't let me."

"I have plenty of friends." He sailed Charlie's book several feet down the hall.

"Maybe, but with the wrong crowd."

Charlie grabbed his book as he hurried to class. He slipped into his seat, glaring at Nate's short spiky hair. *Oh brother, Nate's in the same homeroom with me.*

"Charlie Hooper," Ms. Cone scolded. "You're late. If you make it a habit, it's detention."

He scrunched down in his seat. "Yes, ma'am." *Seventh grade is going to be tough,* he thought.

He glanced over at Rick and Rae. Rick brushed his sandy hair out of his blue eyes. "Sorry," he whispered.

"Me, too." Rae nodded with a friendly smile.

Ms. Cone rapped on her desk. "Class, I would like to introduce to you a new student to Pinesdale Middle School. This is Nancy Mims. Nancy, you may sit in that empty desk in front of Charlie Hooper."

In second period study hall, Charlie scratched his head, trying to concentrate. He fiddled with the collar of his red-plaid shirt.

Mr. Barton came over to his desk and touched him on the shoulder. "Charlie, will you please run an errand for me? Take these forms to the office and give them to Mrs. Pitts personally. They are very important."

"Yes sir, I'll be glad to."

When Charlie entered the school office, he could see Mrs. Pitts, the principal, in her inner office talking to the school security officer.

"I have some important forms for Mrs. Pitts," he told the secretary. "Mr. Barton asked me to give them to her personally."

"Have a seat here. Mrs. Pitts is busy. She'll be with you shortly."

He couldn't help overhearing the conversation between Mrs. Pitts and the officer. "I can't figure out how anyone got into the building. There's been no break-in, nor is anything missing but the computer," Mrs. Pitts said.

"Who has access to the keys?" the officer asked her.

"Well, there's the custodian, Mr. Thomas, Mr. Butler, the P.E. teacher and assistant principal, the school secretary, and myself."

"Are you sure nothing else is missing?"

"I don't think so."

A stolen computer! This could be a serious problem!

"We'll be on the lookout for evidence."

"Thank you for your help."

After he left, Mrs. Pitts came to her door. "Come on in, Charlie. What do you need?"

"Mr. Barton asked me to personally give these forms to you. He said they were important."

"Thanks. You may put them on my desk."

On his way back to the room, he noticed Nate lurking in the hall.

"What are you up to?" he whispered. "Being nosy, I suppose."

"None of your business!" Nate hissed, walking away in a huff.

"Hey, Nancy, come sit with us!" Rae called out to the new girl. She made her way across the noisy crowded lunchroom and set her tray down next to Rae.

Charlie took a gulp from his milk carton and wiped his mouth with his napkin. "Have you heard the latest? Someone stole a computer! And there seems to be no break-in."

Rae stared at him for a moment. "You're kidding. How could anyone have gotten into the building?"

"No strange fingerprints or footprints?" Rick asked.

"Whoever did it must have used gloves and plastic covers over their shoes." Nancy surprised them with her comment.

Before Charlie could answer, he felt a warm glob hit the back of his head and slide down his neck. He reached up to touch it. Gummy spaghetti squished in his hand. "Man, what a mess!" He twirled around, and there was Nate, at the next table, staring him in the face. "You creep! Why did you do that?"

"Bad luck, # 13!" Nate gave him a cocky grin. "Besides, I thought you loved spaghetti."

Rae grabbed a handful of napkins. "Here, Charlie, take these and clean yourself up. Get rid of that nasty stuff. Gross!"

"What were we talking about before Nate's rude interruption?" He wiped the last of the spaghetti from his neck.

"The stolen computer," Rick answered.

"There's something else. I saw Nosy Nate lurking in the hall. He acted strange."

"Really?" Nancy asked.

Charlie winked. "Maybe there's a 'phantom'!"

"And maybe not." Rae grinned.

Later that afternoon, on his way to the gym, Charlie swung his sports bag back and forth. Approaching the computer lab, he discovered Nate, lingering around the crime scene. Charlie ducked out of sight. Tape across the door read, "DO NOT CROSS!" *What could he possibly want here? He can't get in the room.*

Nate glanced around the hall, then bent down and stuck a key in the doorknob. He opened the door a little and started to duck under the tape. *Thud!* Charlie dropped his bag! Startled, Nate shut the door and disappeared down the hall.

How weird is that? Charlie grabbed his bag and headed to class.

"Mom, I'm home!" Charlie called from the treehouse. "Rick and Rae are here, too. Can we have some snacks?"

"Sure, hon, I'll bring them right out. How about some lemonade and cookies?" she asked from the back door. "Let me finish this last line of my column for the *Gazette*."

Charlie Hooper, Detective:

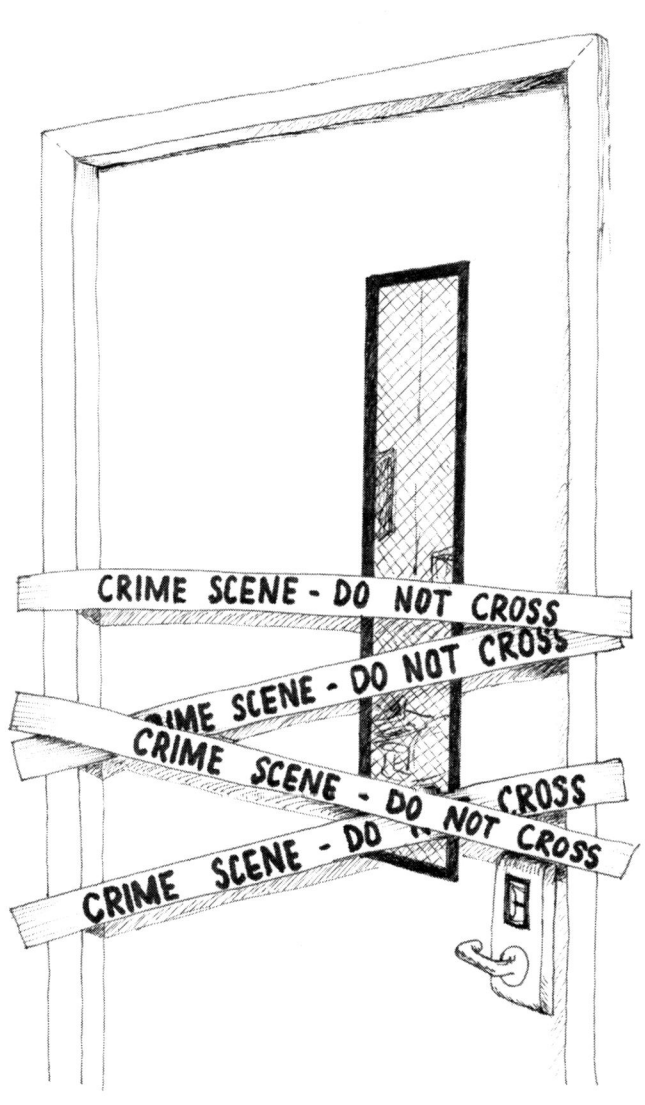

A few minutes later, she called up to him. "Here's your snack. Remember, pull the rope slowly."

"Thanks, Mom." Charlie guided the rope smoothly through the pulley, and the box floated up to the treehouse. He sat back and handed out the snacks.

"What a day!" he sighed. "A terrible locker, Nate all in my face, in trouble with Ms. Cone, and a mystery!"

"Can you believe it? A stolen computer and no break-in?" Rick looked puzzled.

"And did you say Mr. Thomas and Mr. Butler have keys?" Rae asked.

"Could they be suspects?" Rick suggested.

"Maybe," Charlie answered. "I saw the security officer talking to them and they probably both have airtight alibis. Well, there's no such thing as ghosts. So, how was the computer stolen? Something's odd." He reached for another cookie and popped it into his mouth. "Yum! These cookies are great." He gobbled down a couple more.

"How can you think of food at a time like this?" Rae asked.

Charlie shrugged his shoulders and grinned. "Anytime is a good time for food. This sounds like a perfect case for The Pinesdale Sleuths. What do you think?"

"Yeah. Remember how we cracked the case of Mrs. Jameson's missing pearl necklace this summer?" Rae smiled.

"That rocked!" Rick added.

"Yeah, sweet!" Charlie said. "Ol' Sticky-Fingers sure looked sneaky with his twitchy eye, reaching for the metal box of money."

"And what about Doll-Face's thick makeup and frizzy hairdo? What a hoot!" Rae laughed.

"You were so smart to think that Ol' Sticky-Fingers unlocked Mrs. Jameson's window when he went in her house to use the bathroom. I would never have thought about it," Rick said.

"Thanks. It was an idea I got from one of the mystery books I read. Ever since we solved that case, we've been known as The Pinesdale Sleuths."

"Thanks to the newspaper reporter," Rae piped up.

"I *know* we can solve more mysteries." Charlie smiled.

"Charlie," his mom called from the back door. "Rick and Rae need to go home. Their mom just called."

"Okay, Mom."

Rick and Rae stood, gathering their backpacks. Rick grabbed one more cookie. "See ya tomorrow."

"Yeah." Rae waved and started down the ladder. "We'll be thinking about our new case. Maybe one of us will come up with an idea."

"Good. See you two in the morning."

Charlie set his Bible aside and turned off his bedside lamp. He fluffed up his pillow and lay back with his arms crossed behind his head. The moonlight streamed into his room, giving it a soft glow. He thought of the verse he just read, Colossians 4:6. *"Let your conversation be always full of grace, seasoned with salt, so that you may know how to answer everyone."*

Lord, the way I talked to Nate today wasn't gracious at all. Please forgive me for talking to him that way. Help me to live up to Grandpa's advice to always stick by a friend, no matter what.

Chapter 3
THE FLASHBACK

After school the next day, Charlie rushed into the kitchen, grabbed a couple of cookies from the cookie jar, and headed to his treehouse.

I can't get Ol' Sticky-Fingers out of my mind. He gobbled down the cookies and stretched out to think about the case of Mrs. Jameson's missing necklace. The breeze was warm and light. . .

Charlie noticed his elderly neighbor in her yard. She looked worried about something.

"Hi, Mrs. Jameson," he called. "How are you today?"

"Oh, Charlie, I'm so distressed! I've lost my valuable pearl necklace. It was an heirloom handed down from

my great-grandmother and has sentimental value to me."

"When did you lose it?"

"Last Sunday. I know I had it on when I left church. It must've fallen off my neck when I tripped over a root in my yard. The next day, I hired a man to do some yard work. Do you think he might have found it and picked it up?"

"Maybe. Have you reported this to the police?"

"Yes, but they couldn't find enough evidence to make a case. Can you help? You're clever and trustworthy."

"Can you describe the man?"

"Well, it's been a few days," she replied. "Let me think. It seems he was tall and thin, with a slight limp. He had dark eyes. I remember that. Oh, and he had a twitch in one eye."

"Can you remember which leg?"

"No, I'm sorry."

"How about which eye twitched?"

"No, I can't remember that either."

"I'll do my best to solve this case," he told her as he waved goodbye.

Thank you, God, Charlie prayed. *My chance to be a real detective! Maybe Rick and Rae will want to help solve this mystery.*

Charlie waved his hands wildly at Rick and Rae. "Boy, have I got some exciting news for you!" He explained about Mrs. Jameson's mystery.

"You're kidding! You want us to help solve a mystery of a missing necklace?" Rick's eyes lit up.

"Yeah, we'd better get started investigating the neighborhood," Charlie answered. "Maybe someone has seen the yard man."

"We can check at the grocery store," Rae said.

"And we can go to the library," Rick added.

"We'll look for suspects at Pinesdale City Park. Let's get our bikes."

With her mind on the mystery, Rae collided with Mr. Johnson. Oranges, apples, and soda cans tumbled out of his bags.

"Oh, I'm so sorry." She helped him with his groceries. "Have you seen a tall, thin man with a limp?"

"No, I'm afraid not. The police asked me the same question a few days ago. Is he the one who took Mrs. Jameson's necklace?"

Rae nodded. "Maybe. We need to find him."

The friends raced up the steps to the library door. They opened it quietly and searched for the librarian. Charlie approached her as she placed returned books back on a shelf.

"Have you seen a tall, thin man with a limp hanging around in the last few days?" he asked in a soft voice.

"It's hard to say. So many people come and go. I wish I could be of more help."

As the friends arrived at the park, Charlie spotted a tall, thin man clutching a purple pouch. A smug grin spread across the man's face. Charlie started to approach the suspect when he stepped in a hole, fell and hit his head on the corner of a bench.

"O-hh!" Charlie groaned, rolling on the ground.

"Are you okay?" Rick asked.

"Do you think you can stand?" Rae asked with concern in her voice. "Here, let us help you." They got on each side of Charlie and pulled him up by his arms. He raised his head in time to notice the suspect hobbling into an old black car. The car zoomed away, squealing its tires.

"That's great!" Charlie yelled. "He's getting away! And it looks like a woman at the wheel!"

Rae's mouth opened wide. "Wow! Charlie, you really have a whopper!"

Charlie felt the bump on his forehead. "It's not that big. Let's look around town for more clues. I know he was our suspect. He'll probably sell the necklace and skip town. Hey, what's this?" He stooped over, staring at some strange footprints where the suspect stood before taking off in the getaway car. "These look like prints from rain boots. And here's a piece of paper!"

"Why would he wear rain boots?" Rae asked. "It hasn't rained in days."

"Exactly!" Charlie grinned. "That's what's so weird."

"Is there anything on that paper?" Rick asked.

Charlie looked down at it. "Well, you won't believe this. It says, 'Pinesdale Bus Station — locker 229'."

"Maybe he's trying to confuse the police or anyone else on his trail." Rick looked puzzled.

"Well, he's got me confused," Rae agreed.

Rick threw up his hands. "We're doomed. How do we know where the suspects are going?"

"Bingo! I think I might know where they're headed." Charlie motioned. "Remember the old shack near Lark's Lake? Bet that's where they're going. We'll check out the locker later."

"Let's hurry!" Rae raced for her bike.

Hiding their bikes in nearby bushes, they crept up to the run-down shack. There were the shabby black car and the odd footprints of the rain boots.

"Let's sneak closer to that window," Rick whispered.

"Shhh! Listen," Charlie said in a soft voice.

"Is that all you came up with?" the jittery voice growled. Through the window, they could see thick makeup on her full face. Her big hair was frizzy and an odd shade of red.

"I was lucky to get this, Doll-Face," the man replied, holding out the pearl necklace. "What did you want me to do, rob a bank? Then we'd really get caught for good."

"Oh, hush." The woman strutted into another room, slamming the door behind her.

The man slowly lit a huge cigar. As he puffed on the thing, the cigar's smoke drifted through the open window. Inhaling the stink of it, Charlie covered his mouth with his hand to quiet his coughing and gagging.

"Oh, no," Charlie whispered. "Ol' Sticky-Fingers is leaving. We've got to follow him." He ran to the hidden bikes.

"Where do you think he's going?" Rick said.

"He'll probably sell the necklace and skip town with his girlfriend."

"Let's try the pawn shop downtown," Rae suggested. "If we hurry, we might catch him. If not, we might find the necklace."

As they neared Tony's Pawn Shop, the man limped out the door, counting some money.

"Look!" Rick yelled. "There he is!"

"Hey, you! Stop!" Charlie shouted, but the man hopped in a car and got away.

"What will we do now?" Rae asked.

"Let's find out if Tony has the necklace," Charlie said.

Tony stood behind the counter. "May I help you?"

"What did that man sell you?" Charlie asked.

Tony held Mrs. Jameson's pearl necklace in his hand.

"That's it! The lost necklace!" Rae cried.

"This necklace was taken from Mrs. Jameson and should be reported to the police," Charlie explained to Tony.

"Oh, you mean this is the necklace the police are looking for? I'll call them." He began dialing the phone.

"Hey! What about the note?" Rae asked. "What does it mean to the case?"

"What note?" Charlie asked.

"The one you found by the footprints in the park and stuffed in your pocket, Brainy."

"Oh, that note. I remember now." Charlie pulled out the crumpled paper. "It says, 'Pinesdale Bus Station—locker 229'. But how can we get in it? We don't have the key, Smartie."

"We've got to get the key and find out what it has to do with this case," Rick said. "Let's think where the key could be. Maybe Doll-Face or Sticky-Fingers has it."

"If we go to the bus station, we might run into one of them," Rae suggested.

"Come on, let's go." Charlie started in that direction.

Keeping a low profile, the friends slipped through the door of the building. They looked around for anything suspicious.

"Hey, over there!" Charlie pointed. "It's Sticky-Fingers. We'd better hide behind this display." He could still smell the loud stink of the vile cigar.

Sticky-Fingers opened a locker and reached his sneaky hand into it. His eye twitched wildly as he pulled out a small metal container, holding it close to his skinny body.

Charlie elbowed Rick. "Wonder what's in there. He's really acting suspicious."

Rick nodded his head, wide-eyed.

Rae pointed. "We'd better follow him again. He's getting away."

"He's going back to the old shack. Probably for Doll-Face," Charlie said. "Be careful he doesn't see us."

God, please don't let them get away. I am sure glad Mom let me use her cell phone today. *Charlie found the police number in the phone. He punched the call button.*

"Come on, Honey, we got to scram before the police get here," Sticky-Fingers shouted. "I know those pesky kids told them."

After a while, Sticky-Fingers and Doll-Face scrambled out of the shack, loaded with suitcases and bags. Doll-Face bumped the car door, dropping the metal container, and spilling money everywhere.

About that time, sirens wailed and the police surrounded the suspects. "Freeze. Down on your knees, hands behind your head."

"Are we glad to see you!" Charlie and his friends rode up on their bikes.

"Yeah," a police officer said. "Tony at the pawn shop told us that you told him about the pearl necklace. If it hadn't been for you calling us, we wouldn't have caught these crooks. They are slippery as eels. We've *been on their trail for weeks. Mrs. Jameson will be so happy. Congratulations."*

On the evening news, it was reported local children helped apprehend long-sought suspects, Clyde and Chloe Clemens, in the disappearance of a pearl necklace and other valuables. Police say they've accounted for all the missing items.

"Now we're real detectives! We solved our first case!"

Charlie sat up grinning. "It sure would be awesome if we can solve the phantom mystery," he said out loud.

Chapter 4

A Mysterious Clue

After first period, Charlie stood in a daze as he thought about the "phantom". He fumbled with the combination on his locker again. *This is so puzzling. How could anyone steal a computer without keys to the school and the computer lab?*

"Charlie Hooper," the intercom announced, "please come to the office."

"Uh-oh! What've I done now? More bad luck, I suppose," he muttered.

He hesitated at the door of the office. "Did you want to see me, Mrs. Pitts?"

"Yes, Charlie," she answered as she started to sit in her seat. "E-eek!" There, in the middle of her soft flowered cushion, a snake was coiled! It flicked its tongue. She flinched. "Get it out of here! Who would do such a thing?"

Charlie stared at it, astonished. "Don't worry! It's probably not poisonous. I'll get Mr. Thomas. He's sweeping the hall. He's always willing to help."

While Mr. Thomas caught the snake, Mrs. Pitts glanced at her desk. "That's strange! How did my master key get here? I haven't used it in a couple of days." She looked at Charlie with a puzzled expression.

That skunk! Nate Thatcher! He's always pulling pranks. A snake and a key. Just like him.

"You know a computer was stolen yesterday," Mrs. Pitts continued. "The school board and I don't think it'll end here. We need your help."

He looked at her with surprise. "How can I help?"

"I read about Mrs. Jameson's missing necklace in the newspaper this summer. I've already notified the police that The Pinesdale Sleuths might be in on this case. Will you help us?"

"Do the police have any suspects or evidence?"

"Not yet."

"We'll do our best. Is it okay if we start looking for clues?"

"Sure." She nodded, handing him the computer lab key. "You can start after school."

As Charlie walked back toward his locker, he saw Rick and Rae in the hall with Nancy.

"Hey!" he called. "We have a crime to solve!"

"You mean the *computer* crime?" Nancy asked.

"I'll tell you all about it at lunch. We've got to get to class now."

"Great!" Rae said. "See you at lunch."

"I could hardly wait until lunch to hear about your crime solving," Nancy said, before taking a bite of her taco.

"This summer we helped the police solve the mystery of a missing necklace." Charlie told her the whole story.

"As you know, somebody stole a computer," he explained. "Mrs. Pitts wants us to help solve this mystery."

"Really?" Rae squealed. "She wants us to help solve a big case like this?"

"Cool," Nancy said. "I love mysteries. I'm a regular Nancy Drew at heart. I helped solve a midnight burglar mystery."

"A what?" Rick asked.

"There was a burglar who went through our neighborhood robbing people's homes. My friends and I decided we wanted to be a part of capturing him. He would always go into people's back yards and get in that way. We planned a trap, since my house was the only one that hadn't been robbed. We fixed a wire at my back gate and tripped him. One of my friends hit him with a skillet. He was totally stunned. We tied him up, called 9-1-1, and I woke my dad."

"Golly, that was gutsy, Nancy!" Charlie said with admiration.

"Hey, y'all, how about Nancy joining The Pinesdale Sleuths?" Rae asked. "She's great at solving mysteries."

"Yeah," Charlie agreed. "Would you join?"

"Sure. Thanks for making me feel so welcome. I have new friends already."

"By the way," Rick asked, "where do you live?"

"Oh, I live on Birchwood Drive."

Charlie's eyes widened. "Hey, that's a block from me! We always meet at my treehouse to discuss our cases and you'll be close. But today, let's start looking for clues at the crime scene. Meet me by the computer lab after school."

"You got it," Nancy said.

When they got to the computer lab, the yellow tape was still draped across the door.

"Come on," Rick said. "Let's go in."

Without hesitation, Charlie unlocked the door, leaving it slightly open after they entered. The closed-up lab was quiet and neat, as if nothing had happened. The sleuths crept through the room, looking for any clues the police might have missed.

"Look!" Charlie knelt. There, behind a table leg, he spotted a piece of paper folded many times. Carefully unfolding it, he stood. "It says, *'Tonight—10:00 p.m.'!*"

"The computer was stolen yesterday, right?" Nancy asked. "Does it mean 10:00 p.m. yesterday or 10:00 p.m. today?"

"The suspects probably dropped it yesterday, and the police didn't notice during their investigation," Charlie said.

"The robbers might have tried to come back for the note," Rick added.

"I read a mystery one time about some robbers who had a secret hideout." Nancy had a faraway look as she pictured it in her mind.

"Do you think these crooks could have a secret hideout?" Rick asked.

"Hmmm." Charlie nodded. "Maybe they take the stolen items to their hideout at 10:00." He shook his head. "Boy, this is getting complicated."

The door slammed with a bang! "What happened?" Rae asked.

Charlie pushed against it. "The door is jammed! We're trapped! Something weird is going on!"

"What will we do?" Nancy yelled.

The sleuths began screaming for help, pounding on the door. After a while, it burst open. Mr. Thomas came into the room with his broom.

"I heard noise and saw a chair jammed under the doorknob," he said. "Are you kids okay?"

Charlie nodded. "Thanks, Mr. Thomas. We'd better get home."

"I sure am glad Mr. Thomas heard us," Charlie said, walking down Courtwood Drive.

"Yeah, we might have had to spend the night," Rae said.

"We really would have been hungry, and I'm already starving."

"You're right about that. We can hear your stomach growling over here." Rick grinned and the girls giggled.

Gravel sprayed over the friends' shoes as Nate's bike slid to a halt right in front of the group. "Well, if it isn't The Four Musketeers. What adventure are you up to now? Lookin' for an old lady's missing cane this time?"

"Get lost," Charlie said. "Get out of our way. You're just jealous. We have better things to do than talk to you."

"Oh, I have plenty of important things to do, Sherlock. You wouldn't believe the important jobs I have." Nate sneered as he turned his bike and pedaled away.

"What's he talking about?" Rae asked.

"Nate seems to have lots of problems," Nancy said. "He certainly doesn't like you, Charlie."

"No, he doesn't, but that's a long story for another time. Want to come to the treehouse with us?"

Yeah," Rick piped up. "His mom serves great snacks."

"You can call your mom from my house."

Nancy climbed up the ladder. "Wow! This is a *neat* treehouse."

"My dad and grandpa helped me build it. Hurry and pull up the ladder. We don't want Nosy Nate to follow us."

"Bet you had a ball building it," Nancy said.

"We did. But now I'm ready to eat!" Charlie said. "Help yourself, Nancy." He took a big bite out of his brownie.

Carol A. Lanier

"Mmmm, your mom *is* a great cook," she said. "These are delicious."

Charlie and the sleuths gazed out at his two-story white-framed house. Green shutters brightened the windows and baskets of red geraniums hung across the back porch, swaying in the sticky summer breeze.

Charlie couldn't keep his mind on his math homework. Finally, he put his pencil down. The day's unusual events kept whirling around in his head. He wrote as he thought.

1. Snake and key found in Mrs. Pitts' office
2. The sleuths asked to help solve the case
3. Locked in computer lab
4. Note: "tonight—10:00 p.m."

I wonder what Grandpa would do. It was as if he could hear his grandpa's voice. "Charlie, have you prayed about this?" He smiled and sat up straighter in his chair.

God, I did it again. I wasn't very nice to Nate. He really gets on my nerves. Please help me to do better. And God, help me figure out how Grandpa would solve this case. We found a clue, but what does it mean? Who wrote the note and where are they meeting?

Chapter 5

THE HAUNTED MANSION

On Wednesday, Charlie glared at his locker, as usual. *Wonder who locked us in the computer lab and why.* He reached for his math book. *I'd better not be late for class again.*

Rick hit him on the back. "How are things going, pal?" he asked. "I heard some kids saying the old Mason Mansion is haunted. They say the lights turn on and off by themselves. What do you think?"

"You don't really think it's haunted, do you? I know we heard and saw some strange things there, but that doesn't mean it's haunted. I think *people* do the weird stuff. Maybe we need to investigate more."

Rick shook his head. "I don't know about that."

Charlie looked around and there, behind Rick, stood Nate.

"Aw, there's nothing haunted about that dumb place. I've been there. It isn't so scary." Nate shrugged and sauntered away. "Whatever—I wouldn't waste my time," he called over his shoulder.

Between bites of pizza, Charlie and Rick told the girls what the other kids said about the Mason Mansion being haunted.

"Why does anyone think it's haunted?" Rae asked. "It's only superstition."

"Mysterious things happened when we were there," Charlie said. "The dumbwaiter door closed by itself."

"And there was an expensive-looking vase smashed on the floor," Rae added.

"And remember, I saw somebody running from behind the mansion," Charlie said.

"Really?" Nancy raised her eyebrows. "Those *are* all pretty bizarre things."

"We've been so busy solving crimes, I'd forgotten all about the mansion," Charlie remarked. "Why don't we check it out again? We'll explore it after school. Let's meet at the bike rack."

"I haven't seen this place, but count me in," Nancy replied.

"Maybe we can get to the bottom of all this strange stuff," Charlie added.

As the friends approached the run-down Mason Mansion, Charlie noticed several things. Ivy covered the brick walls. Some of the broken windows were boarded up. A black metal fence with a rusty gate surrounded the property. A handwritten sign drooped on the gate that read:

kEEp OUT!

Charlie pointed. "This sign wasn't here before."

"Who wrote it?" Rick asked.

"It's not a real sign. Looks like some crazy kid's writing," Charlie said.

"Do you think it's safe to go in?" Nancy asked.

Carol A. Lanier

"Sure, we'll be fine. Let's go."

The worn floors creaked as they crept inside. Glimmers of light shone through spaces in the boards covering the windows. The loose glass panes rattled with each move they made.

"My grandmother told me this used to be a fancy place," Charlie explained. "She said it was filled with Italian decorations and tile floors. Beautiful crystal chandeliers hung from the ceiling."

"It looks spooky now," Nancy said.

"These mirrors once had beautiful gold frames," he told them.

"They're sure hanging crooked!" Rae exclaimed. "And look how many cracks there are in the mirrors."

"Have you heard about the legend?" Charlie asked. "It tells of smugglers hiding their valuable loot in a secret room years ago."

"I knew there had to be a secret room!" Nancy shouted. "How exciting!"

"It's said thieves stashed their valuables in the secret room and left them there until the right time to move them," he said mysteriously. "Hmmm, do you think the robbers might bring the stolen computer here?"

"Could it be why the lights go on and off?" Nancy asked.

"Cool!" Rick said. "Maybe that's why some kids think the place is haunted."

"Ooh! This place is creepy!" Rae shivered. "There are cobwebs hanging from the lights and spiders crawling everywhere. I don't want any spiders falling on me!"

"Yuck! You're right." Nancy looked all around.

Squeeak!

Rae grabbed Charlie's arm and whispered, "Is someone else in here?"

Suddenly, a door flung open. A man stared at them in surprise. He almost knocked Charlie down as he dashed toward the front door.

"Did you get a good look at his face?" Charlie asked.

"Not really." Rick shuddered. "He had gray hair and a beard."

"And a greenish tattoo on his arm," Rae added.

"He was strange-looking," Nancy said.

Charlie looked puzzled. "Wonder where he came from and what he was doing."

"Maybe he's a thief, like the legend told," Rae teased. "Or, maybe he's the same person you saw last time."

"Or, maybe the mansion *is* haunted," Rick said.

"As much as the man scared me, I don't think he was a ghost." Nancy crossed her arms.

"Let's investigate and see where he came from," Charlie suggested.

Rick stepped into a dusty room. "Get a load of this."

Rae pointed to some shelves. "Look at these old books."

"This must be the library. I bet you could keep a ton of mysteries in here," Nancy said.

"Wait a minute. Here's a door. Where does it lead?" Charlie tried to turn the doorknob, but it wouldn't budge. "Come on, Rick, help me give it a push. One, two, three!" Their shoulders shoved with force. "Okay, again. One, two, three!" It still didn't give. They took a few steps back. Charlie counted again and they gave it another mighty push. Nothing. "Try kicking it. One, two, three!" They raised their feet, striking the door firmly.

"It's either locked or a dead-end," Rae said. "Let's go."

Charlie snapped his fingers. "No, there might be a key! My grandmother always kept door keys on the doorframe. Give me a boost, Rick." He put his foot in Rick's laced hands and stretched up to feel. "Sweet! Look what I found!" He jumped down, holding an old-fashioned silver key.

"Do you think it'll fit?" Nancy asked.

"Try it," Rae said.

"I'm not sure I want to go in there." Nancy stepped back. "It might be scary. What if another man jumps out?"

Charlie stuck the key in, turned it, and heard a grating sound. He tried the doorknob, and the door swung open with a squeak.

"Hurry up, Charlie." Rae gave him a little push.

"This *is* big," he said, moving toward the open door across the room. "Wonder what it was used for."

"Hey, don't leave me behind." Nancy followed them. "I'm not staying here by myself." She looked up at the ceiling. "I can just see those two chandeliers over a long dining table. A huge one seating twenty people."

"I think you're right," Charlie said. "This little room back here, with the shelves, leads to the kitchen, so this must be the dining room."

"Whoa! Hold on, y'all—a picture of a woman and a little girl." Rick leaned over to pick it up off the dusty floor.

"Oh, it's an *old* picture," Rae said.

Charlie took the photo, turned it over and read:

Lucy and Corinna Mason
Corinna—age 5

"Why did they leave this picture?" Rae asked. "They must have been some of the Masons who lived here. I wonder how long ago."

"What's that in the background?" Nancy pointed. "An antique chest? Where you keep silverware? This picture must've been taken right here in the dining room."

"Bet it *is* a silver chest," Charlie said. "Wonder what happened to it. We'll investigate more another time. We have to go now."

When they approached the foyer to leave, they heard a muffled sound.

"Shhh!" Charlie put his finger to his lips.

Rae asked in a soft voice, "Is it the same man?"

They heard the muffled noise again. A swaying white figure stepped awkwardly down the wide curved stairway.

"Let's hide behind this door and watch," Rick said, pulling Rae back.

Rae giggled as she winked at Nancy. "Its feet look peculiar." The "ghost" was wearing sneakers with blue and red striped socks.

"I've never seen a 'ghost' in shoes and socks," Nancy whispered.

Charlie and Rick ran up to the "ghost" and snatched off the white sheet. "Look," Charlie shouted. "It's Nate Thatcher! Thought you wouldn't waste your time in this place."

"I was only joking," Nate said. "I was trying to scare you. Can't you take a joke? I know you thought it was funny."

"Yeah, can't you see us rolling on the floor, laughing?" Rae asked.

"Will you ever stop pulling pranks?" Charlie asked. "They aren't always funny. Sometimes they're mean."

"Yeah, yeah, yeah, so you say, loser." Nate shoved his hands in his pockets and then slowly left the mansion with a smug look on his face.

"Nate sure is acting freaky," Charlie said. "Did you see that big grin, Rick? He looked like the cat that swallowed the canary. Guess we did solve the mystery of the Mason Mansion 'ghost'!" The sleuths hooted with laughter.

But can we solve the case of the school "phantom"? And who was that man?

Back in his treehouse, Charlie thought about how mean Nate was to others, but he also remembered his grandpa's advice.

Carol A. Lanier

God, I know I'm to be a friend to Nate. But why is he always cooking up trouble? It sure makes it hard to be his friend.

Chapter 6

Nosy Nate

Crash! Something hit the floor! Charlie turned around, twisting his neck for a better look. He poked Rick. "Uh-oh! Nate's at it again."

There stood Nancy, with her tray and food all over the floor—hamburger, mustard, ketchup, and French fries—all smeared in a slippery mess.

With hands on hips, she wrinkled her brow. "Look what you did, you bully!"

"Watch out!" a boy called. "Don't step on the greasy hamburger or the ooey-gooey mustard and ketchup."

"Will Nate ever stop horsing around?" Charlie asked Rae, irritated.

She rushed to help Nancy. "Are you okay?" Rae gave Nate a stern look. "Let's get another tray and hurry back to our table."

"Hey, Nancy, don't mind Nate," Rick said. "He's a real jerk."

"Yeah, I can see that!" Nancy made a face. "All that food on the floor makes me lose my appetite."

"You need to eat a little," Charlie coaxed.

After Nancy finished her hamburger, Rae motioned for her to put up their trays. "Come on. Let's get going to history class."

"See you guys later." Nancy waved.

Halfway down the hall, Nancy came to a halt, pulling Rae back. "Look! Isn't that the strange man we saw at the mansion?" She shuddered. "He's scary-looking!"

"You're right. And there's Nate handing him a bag. What's in it? Why are they meeting at school? Let's sneak in here and see if we can hear what they're saying." Rae grabbed Nancy's hand, darting into the girl's restroom. They peeked around the door, watching Nate and the man.

"This isn't much, Nate," the older man told him, as he peered into the bag. "We need lots more. You've got to do better if you know what's good for you."

"I'll do b-b-better," he stuttered, with a frightened look on his face.

"See that you do!" The man stormed away.

They watched Nate walk down the hall. "He really looks scared," Nancy whispered. "Even though I don't like him, I hope he'll be okay."

"We'd better tell the boys about this," Rae replied. "I'm curious about what was in the bag."

After school, the sleuths met in the treehouse. The boys sat speechless while the girls told their story. "That *is* a real mystery," Charlie agreed, baffled.

When his friends left, Charlie went straight to his room. A sign hung on the door that read:
CHARLIE HOOPER
DETECTIVE AT WORK!
DO NOT DISTURB
I have some deep thinking to do. He plopped down on his bed. *God, something strange is going*

on at school. *Why was Nate talking to that man, and what was in the bag? What would Grandpa do?*

After study hall the next day, Charlie headed straight to math class. He stopped dead in his tracks. "Not Nate again!" he groaned with aggravation.

"Well, if it isn't Sherlock Holmes," Nate joked, standing right in front of him. "Where's Watson?"

Charlie didn't answer. He started to go around Nate, but Nate blocked him again.

"Get out of my way, Nate!"

"Sure, Sherlock."

Charlie walked on to class, furious at Nate. *One of these days, you're really going to get it! Thank goodness it's Friday. No Nate for two whole days!*

Charlie made it to his seat before the bell rang. "Whew!" he whispered to Rae and Rick. "Made it on time!"

Nancy smiled. "Good for you!"

Ms. Cone told the class to take out their math assignment. Without warning, a slimy green blob splattered on the chalkboard. Her face turned beet-red with fury. She noticed Nate hide something in his desk. His hands were pea-green and he slouched lower in his seat.

"Nate Thatcher!" She raised her voice, dropping the book on her desk. "You're in big trouble!" She quickly wrote a note. "Rick, please take this to the office and tell them I need help immediately."

"Sure, Ms. Cone."

As Rick left the room, the class roared with laughter.

"Now you're goin' to get it!"

"Way to go, Nate!"

In a few minutes, Mrs. Pitts stood at the door. "Nate, come with me."

"Okay, class." Ms. Cone sighed. "Nate won't be in our way for a while. Back to work. Please excuse the interruption."

Thank goodness! What a troublemaker.

Later in the afternoon, when Charlie turned the corner of the gym, Mr. Butler almost bumped into him. He was squinting his eyes, trying to read a yellow sticky note. He looked nervous. Charlie could see something light green had spilled on the paper.

Wonder what's in the note, and why is he so nervous, anyway?

On his way to the library, a voice startled Charlie.

"Bein' nosy yourself, huh?"

I'd know that voice anywhere. "What do you want, Nate?" he snapped.

"You had better stop snoopin' around if you know what's good for you," Nate threatened with a hard look on his face.

Charlie flashed a smirk at him. "I'm shaking in my boots."

"You'd better watch it, Charlie."

"Or what?"

"How about we finish this outside?"

"Fighting isn't going to solve anything. You know that."

"Then stop being such a nosy snoop." Nate glared at him, clenching his fists and walking away.

Rae stood beside Charlie at the bookshelf as he reached for a book called *Paleontology and Bones*. "What are you doing your science research paper about?" she whispered. "I can't decide." She followed him back to the table where Nancy and Rick were already seated.

"Skeletons and fossils are awesome," he remarked. "I'm going to write about paleontologists, their digs and findings."

"Hmm, sounds exciting," Nancy said. "Maybe I'll write a paper on Louis Pasteur."

"I love gems," Rae replied. "They're beautiful! I think I'll research rubies."

"I like rocks," Rick said. "Geology is cool."

Charlie started working on his notes. He sensed someone standing right behind him. It was Nate peering over him. "Looking for something?" Charlie asked suspiciously.

"Nope. Do you need help finding Nancy Drew?"

"Beat it, Nate," he whispered.

Out of the corner of his eye, he saw Nate slowly edging over to the coin collection. *What does he have up his sleeve now?*

Charlie remembered Pinesdale Middle had received the coin collection from the Savannah History Museum. Since the museum had closed recently for repairs, they made loans of small exhibits to various schools around the state. Seventh grade history students would be writing reports about the coins. They were part of the artifacts found by archaeologists in 2003 from a vessel that sank off the coast of Georgia in the 1800s.

Suddenly, a loud noise broke the quietness of the library. Charlie's heart pounded as he turned around to see what happened. Wood, glass and coins were scattered on the floor all around the display table.

Mrs. Acres came running from the other side of the library and stopped by Charlie's chair. "What happened here?"

"It was an accident, Mrs. Acres," Nate spoke up. "I leaned too hard on the case looking at the coins. I'm really sorry."

"Charlie, you can help me get this cleaned up," Mrs. Acres said. "Be extra careful of the broken glass. I don't want anyone to get hurt. Only pick up the coins that don't have glass mixed with them. Mr. Thomas can clean up the rest."

He scrambled from his seat and began collecting the coins. "We'll need a box to put them in. The display case is totally wrecked."

"Here, try this box," Mrs. Acres suggested, taking it out of a cabinet. "It has a key and can be locked. We can't let anything happen to the borrowed coins."

"I'll help, too, Mrs. Acres," Nate said, stepping in front of Charlie as he took the box from her. "I'm really sorry." He scooped up a handful of coins.

"Nate, open up the box so we can put these in," Charlie said.

Nate opened it. "Here you go."

"Do you have the key, Mrs. Acres?" Charlie brought the box to her. "We better lock them up."

Mrs. Acres looked frantically around for the key. "It was in the lock of the box. I saw it."

"I don't see a key anywhere on the floor," Rick said. "What happened to it?"

"Yes, it *is* puzzling. I suppose we can put the box in the workroom," Mrs. Acres suggested. "The workroom door locks, and it will be safe there."

Nate wrapped the tail of his shirt over his hand. "Ow!" he cried out. "I cut my finger! It's bleeding. Can I go to the nurse?"

"Sure," Mrs. Acres said. "Wrap this tissue around your finger. Nancy, go with him."

The closer Nate came to the nurse's office, the slower he walked.

"Scared of the nurse?" Nancy asked.

"No, I'm looking for Mr. Thomas."

Just then, he saw him coming down the hall. "Hey, Mr. Thomas. There's been an accident in the library. Nancy'll show you."

When they were out of sight, Nate stuffed the tissue in his jingling pocket and whistled as he walked down the hall.

Back at the library, Mr. Thomas spoke to Mrs. Acres. "Nate said you needed help. An accident happened?"

"Yes, the coin display broke and there's glass everywhere. Thanks for coming."

When Nancy returned to the library, she whispered to Charlie. "Nate sure acted weird going to the nurse. He walked really slow."

"Sounds like Nate all right." *An accident? I don't think so. Nate has really been acting suspicious. I know he's up to no good.*

"Mom, I'm home! Got something to eat?"

"Sure, Charlie," she said, looking up from her computer. "There are some oatmeal cookies, but we're all out of milk. How about running down to the store for me? Then you can eat your snack when you get back. I've got to finish this article about Mrs. Brock's ninetieth birthday."

"Sure, Mom. I love milk with oatmeal cookies." Charlie took the money she handed him, crammed it in his pocket, and went out to his bicycle. Pedaling along Courtwood Drive on his way to the store, he started thinking about Nate again.

Chapter 7

ANOTHER HEIST

In the quiet of the moonlit night, two prowlers nervously turned the key in the gym door at Pinesdale Middle School. The door shut with an almost silent softness. They went through the gym and entered the main school. The halls were dark except for the faint light of their flashlights and the red glow of the exit signs. The whispering wind scraped the tree branches on the windowpanes, making eerie noises. Terrifying shadows shifted on the walls. The prowlers whirled around.

"What was that?" the short guy asked.

"Oh, probably the wind moving the trees. Come on, we don't have all night," the tall man answered.

Carol A. Lanier

Whoo! Whoo! An owl hooted, sending shivers up their spines. They hurried down the main hall.

The tall man unlocked the library door. "Where did you say they put the box?"

"I heard them say in the workroom. Your key should open it. I have the key to the box." The shorter one shined his flashlight around to spy for more valuables. "What are these shiny things on the floor under this cabinet? They look like some of the coins." He squatted down to pick up the coins and started to put them in his pocket.

"Hey, let me have those. Give me the key to that box, too."

Crack! The smaller fellow bumped a framed picture on the wall, causing it to slide to the floor. One corner of the frame broke.

"You really are clumsy. Mr. Thomas has already cleaned up after your escapade Friday. Now what are we going to do? We don't have the materials to fix it. They'll suspect something for sure."

"I'll hang it back on the wall and kick this piece under the cabinet. No one will even notice it." He whirled around. "I hear something that sounds like a police siren! Is it coming this way?"

"Hurry! We've got to get the box and get out of here. We can't get caught! Help me carry it to the gym. Quick! Turn off your flashlight."

Both lights went out. The room became dark. Feeling their way to the workroom, they grabbed the box, locked the workroom and library doors, and rushed to the gym. The tall man locked the box in a filing cabinet. As the front door of the school opened, the gym door closed with a soft click.

Posters of well-known detectives filled the bright blue walls of Charlie's room. Sherlock Holmes, Colombo, the Hardy Boys, and his grandpa were among his favorites. Various mystery books sat neatly on his desk.

Charlie lay on his bed Monday morning, gazing at the posters while thinking about the few flimsy clues he had. *How would Grandpa have solved this case?* He went over the list of clues in his mind:

1. *Not enough evidence from police, no break-in or prints*

2. *Note in computer lab*

3. *Locked in computer lab. Someone doesn't want us snooping!*

4. *Mr. Butler's curious note*

5. *Nate's strange actions*

6. *Master key appears on Mrs. Pitts' desk, but how and why?*

He jumped up from the bed, throwing on his faded jeans and blue T-shirt. He scrambled down the stairs, two at a time, smelling the sizzling bacon and hot blueberry waffles.

"Mom, this is an awesome breakfast, but I have to get going. I'll be late." Charlie hugged her, grabbing a waffle and a piece of bacon.

On his way to homeroom, Charlie heard a shrill cry from the library. He started in that direction, when he saw a strange gray-haired man in the hall.

That man looks familiar, but I can't figure out why. Where have I seen him?

When he reached the library door, Mrs. Acres threw her hands up in bewilderment. "Oh, Charlie, someone's stolen the coin collection! I know we locked it in the workroom Friday!"

His heart beat faster. *Another heist! Could the stranger be involved?* "Mrs. Acres, did someone call the police? Did they check out the building?"

"Yes, someone reported seeing flashes of lights and shadowy figures. When the police looked everything over, all was clean as a whistle and shipshape. Those were their exact words. However, the police didn't know about the box of coins locked in the workroom."

Mrs. Acres stared at the wall behind him. "Charlie, do you know what happened to this picture? It's on the floor and a corner of the frame is broken. I don't remember that."

"The last time I was in the library, the picture was hanging on the wall," he replied. "I don't have a clue what happened."

By then, Mrs. Pitts and the police arrived. Charlie told them about the stranger. As he turned away, he saw Rick, Nancy and Rae standing at the library door.

"What's going on?" Rick whispered.

"It's another heist," Charlie answered. "The coin collection! Something fishy is definitely going on here. I know there were prowlers over the weekend."

Football banners and posters plastered the cafeteria walls. Charlie wadded his napkin. "Let's go check out the football schedule." He stood. "It's posted outside the gym."

"Cool idea," Rick agreed. "We can see when the first game will start."

"We've been so busy solving this mystery, I really haven't thought about the football games," Charlie said.

"Our team won the regional championship last year," Rae explained to Nancy.

"Really? That's awesome!"

"Let's all go to the first game together," Charlie said.

"Great!" Rae clapped.

As they neared the gym, loud voices bellowed from inside. They glanced through the open door, and noticed Nate and Mr. Butler arguing furiously.

"You fumbling…" snapped Mr. Butler, his pockets jingling. "Let's take this to the drop-off point at…"

"Do you know what they're talking about?" Charlie asked.

Rae and Nancy shook their heads.

"What do they mean by a drop-off point?" Rick asked. "And what's that jingling sound?"

"Boy! They're sure mad!" Rae said.

"Do you think they're working together?" Charlie asked.

Coming back from the gym, Rick tugged at Charlie's arm. "Stop! There's Nate."

Nate hardly noticed them as he hurried past, glaring at a stained note with a strange look on his face.

"What's the smudge on Nate's jeans?" Charlie asked.

"Don't know. Does it matter?" Rick asked.

"It does if it's what I think it is." Charlie grinned. "I think we have *two* phantoms!"

The next morning, in the empty hallway, Nancy opened her locker to find her math book. Without a sound, a hand covered her mouth with tape. Someone dragged her to the broom closet and wrapped more tape around her wrists and ankles. It was dark, dirty, and scary. Nancy tried making noises, but she knew no one could hear her.

In class, Rae waited. "Charlie, have you seen Nancy this morning? She's late and that's not like her."

"No," he said. "Maybe she's absent. Let's ask Ms. Cone."

After math class, the sleuths told Ms. Cone about their concern.

"I'll notify the office," she told them. "I'm sure everything's okay."

At lunch, they still hadn't heard from Nancy. "I'm really worried. The office called home, but no one answered." Rae poked at her food with her fork. "Where is she?"

"Do you suppose something bad happened to her, like being kidnapped?" Rick spoke up.

"It's not likely, but possible with all the strange things going on lately," Charlie answered.

Carol A. Lanier

"But where would the kidnappers keep her? The mansion? Or here at school?" Rae put her chin in her hand to think.

"If Nosy Nate has anything to do with it, I bet she's hidden somewhere here at school," Charlie said. "Let's look around and make sure she's not right under our noses."

"Yeah, we have time before our next class," Rick added. "Let's start at our lockers and walk all the halls. We can look in every room we pass."

In the second hall, they walked past the broom closet. "Wait a minute." Rae put her hand up to stop Charlie. "Wait a minute. I think I hear something."

"I heard it, too. There it is again! A tapping noise." Charlie threw open the unlocked door.

"Mmm, mmm!" Nancy struggled to talk, squirming to get loose.

"What happened?" Rae asked, carefully pulling the tape from her mouth.

"I guess I got kidnapped, even if it wasn't for long," Nancy said in tears. "Boy, was I scared. But I'm sure glad to see you. I tried and tried to make noise, but no one heard me."

"Are you really okay?" Rae clasped her hand.

"Yeah, but I sure don't want to get kidnapped again!"

"Who would do such a thing and why?" Rick asked.

"Maybe they think we know too much and want to scare us," Charlie replied.

"I didn't see anybody," Nancy said. "It happened so fast."

"Maybe it was the 'phantoms'." Charlie smiled. "We'd better report this to Mrs. Pitts."

As the friends headed toward the school office, Charlie said, "Let's celebrate our finding Nancy by going to the Dairy Delite after school for milkshakes. What do you think?"

"Charlie, you're always hungry!" Nancy laughed. "But a chocolate milkshake is just what I need to calm my nerves!"

Music was playing when the sleuths walked through the door of the Dairy Delite. They ordered their shakes and then grabbed their favorite booth.

"This milkshake is delish," Nancy told the others. "I love chocolate."

"Are you feeling any better?" Rae patted her hand.

"Yeah, I guess so, but what a scary experience," she said. "I'm so glad you all are my friends."

"Don't worry," Charlie assured her. "We'll solve this case yet."

That night, when Charlie said his prayers, he included one for Nate. *God, I feel sorry for him. If he hung out with a better crowd, he'd probably act different. It's almost impossible to be his friend.*

Chapter 8

More Puzzling Clues

"We need to investigate the library for more clues," Charlie told the others Wednesday morning before school began. He glanced around the hall to see if the coast was clear. No one was in sight, so they opened the door and darted inside.

Charlie pointed. "Look. Over there. Something's glowing in the sunlight." On the floor, near the coin display table, glistened a tiny speck. They peered down for a closer look.

"I don't see anything," Rick said. "Maybe it's a reflection from a piece of glass."

"Hold on a minute." Charlie pulled a magnifying glass from his backpack. "A Christmas gift from

Mom. She told me every good detective needs a magnifying glass."

"What is it?" Nancy asked in a quiet voice.

"Looks the same as the smudge on Nate's jeans, but much smaller."

"Is the speck paint?" Rae asked. "They've painted the gym. The painters finished last Friday."

"You're right," Charlie agreed. "We had gym class outside most of last week. This looks like the same light-green stuff on Nate's and Mr. Butler's notes. It's paint from the gym!"

"But how does it connect with the robberies?" Rick asked. "What are they doing with the stolen goods?"

"Maybe the speck came from Nate's shoe," Charlie said. "He had paint on his jeans and shoes."

"On the news last night, I heard about a drug ring," Nancy replied. "It's thought to be responsible for other robberies in town. Is it possible these thieves are involved?"

"We don't know for sure," Rae answered. "We'll need more evidence."

"Yeah," Rick agreed. "We've got to come up with more clues."

"When we do get our proof, the culprits will be cooked crooks!" Charlie grinned.

That afternoon, as the four gathered at their lockers, a loud argument began. Seth Sikes stood with his back to them. Nate shoved Seth, knocking him to the floor.

"You liar!" Nate yelled.

"What did Seth say?" Charlie asked. "I couldn't hear him."

"You'll be sorry if you do!" Nate shouted, storming off in anger.

"Are you okay?" Charlie asked, pulling Seth up by his arm.

"Sure," Seth said, trembling. "Nate's a little weird."

"And the class bully," Rae added.

"If you ask me, he's a mean dude!" Rick exclaimed.

"And he's scary!" Nancy shivered.

"I may have a clue to the school mystery," Seth whispered, "but I'm not sure it's important."

"Tell us," Charlie said.

"Monday, I saw Nate with Mr. Butler. They were carrying something into the storage room in the gym. I don't know for sure what it was, but they seemed very secretive about what they were doing. I only got a glimpse of some kind of box. The bad thing is, Nate got a look at me in the doorway. That's what our fight was about. I confronted him and told him I was going to tell someone. You saw and heard the rest."

"Thanks, Seth. This is a great clue." *What's going to happen next?* Charlie wondered.

When the bell rang, the sleuths hurried to pack their backpacks and meet at the treehouse.

"Oh, no! I forgot my science notes. I'll catch up later." Charlie turned back toward his locker. Once there, he struggled with the lock, becoming frustrated.

A voice next to him said, "Here, let me try."

Turning, he saw Nate standing beside him.

"I'm not telling you my combination."

"Stand back." Nate took hold of the lock. "I don't need it." He slipped a thin odd-shaped piece of metal into the base of its post. He gave it a twist. The lock popped open.

Charlie looked puzzled. "How did you do that?"

"Oh, it's easy when you're used to it." A piece of paper slipped from Nate's hand onto the floor. Without noticing it, he reached into the locker for Charlie's notes. "Here. Isn't this what you're looking for? You better get going and catch up with your friends. Aren't you in a hurry?"

"Thanks, Nate."

Nate turned away to his own locker. Charlie could tell he was looking for something. Nate searched in a frenzy, turning his pockets inside out, searching his locker, his backpack, and then his locker again.

"What's wrong? Did you lose something?"

"I had a piece of paper with my homework assignments written on it. Now I can't find it. Mr. Barton and Ms. Cone will really be mad if I don't turn in my homework. It's disappeared and I don't see it anywhere."

"I can give the assignments to you," Charlie offered.

"I'm in a real hurry. I gotta go." Nate slammed his locker and rushed down the hall.

As Charlie turned to leave, he saw a piece of paper on the floor. *Must be some of my science notes.* He bent over, picked up the paper and stuffed it into his backpack.

When Charlie caught up with his friends, he reported the incident. "Nate's acting strange again. He actually seemed nice and opened my locker for me. But he sure looked worried when he couldn't find his homework assignments. Since when has he cared about his homework? I offered to give them to him, but he ran off."

"Charlie, what's that sticking out of your backpack?" Nancy tugged at the zipper.

He slipped the bag off his shoulders, unzipped it, and pulled out a folded piece of paper. "What's this? Maybe Nate's homework assignments." Charlie unfolded it and read. With a stunned expression, he looked at them. "This isn't assignments! It says, 'Nate—meet at boathouse 3:00 p.m. — L'."

"Where's the boathouse and who is 'L'?" Nancy asked.

"Remember the lake behind the mansion? I think the note is talking about the one there. A boathouse and a pier are on one side and a pier and a gazebo are on the other. I just don't know who 'L' is."

"If we hurry, we can get there before Nate and spy on them," Rick said. "Let's get to the lake the back way."

The sleuths hid their bikes in the tall weeds that grew behind the gazebo.

"Why is that SUV parked in these woods?" Rick asked.

Charlie shrugged his shoulders. "I don't know. Let's hide behind these big bushes so we can watch the boathouse and pier. It's almost 3:00, but I don't see anyone. Oh, wait, I see people now. Notice how some of the boards on the pier look new? I think someone has been patching it."

"What for?" Rick asked.

"I think we're about to find out."

Rick pulled his binoculars from his backpack. "Looks like they're loading boxes into a boat. And there's Nate! But now they're walking back toward the mansion."

"We won't be able to see what they're doing," Rae said.

"Why do they need a boat?" Charlie asked. "I've got to get a closer look. Rick, you keep watch with your binoculars. I'm going to swim over to the boathouse. If there's a problem, you and the girls get help."

"What if they come back and you get caught?" Rae asked. "Are you sure you can swim that far?"

"I took an advanced swimming class at summer camp a couple of years ago. I learned to swim like a fish."

Charlie removed his shirt, pocketknife, shoes and socks, handed them to Rae, and then waded into the lake. As the water reached his waist, he began swimming with smooth strong strokes that propelled him quickly. Almost at the shore, he saw the men coming back down the path loaded with boxes. Charlie took a deep breath and disappeared under the water. He resurfaced beneath the pier just as the group stepped into the boathouse.

Charlie Hooper, Detective:

While the men were inside, Charlie slipped out of the water under the drooping branches of a huge weeping willow tree. He stayed out of sight when the group came out onto the pier.

"This load is enough for one trip, Lefty. Nate, you go with him. I'll bring a few more boxes down and have them here when you get back."

Thud. Charlie heard them loading the boxes into the boat. *What is in those boxes? Drugs, maybe?*

"Hurry! Get in, Nate." Lefty gave him a shove. "We've got to get these boxes unloaded at the gazebo and delivered to the boss."

Nate climbed in the front of the boat. The one called Lefty sat in the back and started the motor. It sputtered to life.

Charlie quivered, waving his hands wildly at Rick, pointing to the boat.

"He's trying to warn us about something," Rick cautioned. "We better stay out of sight."

"What about Charlie?" Nancy asked. "Will he be okay?"

"He's a clever guy," Rick said. "He'll think of something."

While the boat puttered across the lake, Charlie hurried out from under the willow tree. He went into the boathouse and saw it empty except for an old rowboat tied to a post and several sealed boxes stacked along the side. He stared at them.

I'd love to see what's in those boxes. If only I had my pocketknife, I might be able to find out. But what if the man comes back? God, please tell me what to do. How do I get back to the others?

He stepped out of the boathouse, looking up the path toward the mansion. It was empty, so Charlie started walking through the woods as fast as he could on his bare feet.

When he found his friends near the gazebo, he asked, "What happened to Nate and the other guy? They called him Lefty!"

"So Lefty is 'L'!" Rae exclaimed.

"They unloaded the boxes into the SUV and took off," Rick said.

"Did you get a good look at the tag number?" Charlie asked.

Rick smacked his forehead. "Duh! I didn't even think about that!"

"Golly, Charlie, we weren't thinking," Nancy said. "Sorry."

"That's okay. We've got to find out more about what they're doing and what's in those boxes. Let's head back to the treehouse."

Chapter 9

IN DISGUISE

The Pinesdale Sleuths gathered in their secret place to discuss their next move.

"What was Nate doing there?" Charlie asked. "We need to keep an eye on him."

"I've heard him say he works out at Sam's Gym after school every Thursday," Rick replied. "Maybe we can meet there about 3:00 and follow him."

"Can you come, Nancy?" Rae asked.

"Oh, I'm sure my mom will let me sleuth with my friends for a while after school." She smiled with a twinkle in her hazel eyes.

"Man, we've been waiting forever." Charlie sighed. "We know he went in, so he's got to come out. What's keeping him?"

"You know the stocky fella that left the gym with the kooky bushy hair and backward baseball cap?" Rick asked. "Something was funny and familiar about him."

Charlie's face lit up as bright as a light bulb. "A disguise!" he shouted. "Nate must be wearing a disguise!"

"Come on. Let's find him," Rae said.

Nancy pointed to a figure by a newspaper stand on the corner. "Is that him?"

There stood the stocky guy facing the Martin Museum. He started across the street with a walk as awkward as a duck, darting in front of cars. Horns blared and people stared at him.

"I'd know his walk anywhere," Charlie said. "It's Nate, for sure! He's wearing a wig!"

"We'd better get going," Rick urged. "We can't lose him."

Nate dashed inside the museum. As he moved into the first display room, the sleuths followed and peeked around the corner. Straight in front of Nate hung a beautiful painting. He made a curious smirk with his lips.

Charlie and his friends watched Nate's every move, trying to keep out of sight. *Snap!* "Good thing I remembered my camera," Rae said.

After a few minutes, Nate hurried out of the museum.

"Where is he going now, and why all the rush?" Charlie asked. "We'd better keep following him."

Outside, Nate stopped by the side of the building. The sleuths ducked down behind the concrete railing of the steps, peeking over the top.

"What's he doing?" Nancy asked.

Nate took something black out of his shirt pocket. He bent over with his back to them. When he straightened and turned around, he looked like an older man.

Rick raised his eyebrows. "A mustache."

Charlie motioned. "This way, y'all."

Nate turned right on Maple Street, and then right again on Oakside Drive. The sleuths followed him but kept their distance. Nate entered Jenkins' Jewelry, looking around with a smug look. The friends peered in through the front window, ready to drop out of sight if Nate should look their way.

"Nancy, why don't you go in and pretend you're shopping for something?" Rae asked. "You can tell us what Nate's doing."

"Sure thing." She slipped into the store and went to a display of watches, careful to keep her back to Nate. She saw him in the mirrors that lined the store behind the counters.

"May I help you, sir?" the clerk asked Nate.

"No, thank you. I'm looking for a birthday gift."

Completely focused, inspecting all the jewelry counters, Nate scribbled fast with a stubby pencil. Slipping the little notepad into his pocket, he left.

Nancy joined her friends at their hiding place around the corner. As they followed Nate, she told them what she saw and heard. "Nate told the clerk he was looking for a birthday present. He was actually writing on a notepad. Can you believe it?"

Nate walked to the old industrial end of town, where empty warehouses stood. He went to the last one in the row.

Charlie pointed. "There's only one way in—through that metal door."

"What would he be doing in an empty warehouse?" Rick asked. "It hasn't been used in years."

Nate tapped three times on the door, and then slipped inside. Charlie ran to the door. He caught it before it closed all the way.

"Come on, y'all," Rick whispered. "We've got to find out what's happening, too."

They stepped into the warehouse, where they heard voices in the back. A fan hummed somewhere close by. Only Nate's voice was familiar. Stepping nearer, the sleuths heard the robbers speaking of taking the stolen items to the mansion. Rae closed the door silently. *Bump!* Her dangling camera hit the wall!

"What's that noise, Joe?" Lefty asked.

"Shhhh!" Charlie whispered. "Over here, behind these tall boxes. We can't let them see us."

"Oh, nothing," Joe answered. "Probably a small box fell. Nate, did you scan the museum and the jewelry store?"

"Boy, did I!"

"Anything worth our trouble?" Lefty asked.

"You bet!"

"We'll make our hit tonight and take the stuff to the mansion," Joe said. "The boss wants us to transfer those goods to the warehouse Friday night, and get them ready to be moved."

"I knew something strange was going on at the mansion," Charlie whispered.

"They probably stash the stolen items in the secret room, just like the legend," Nancy replied.

"Rick, do you recognize those two guys?" Charlie asked.

"Only Nate and Lefty."

"So the man we saw at the mansion isn't one of these men?"

"I don't see him," Rick said.

"Well, there's not much we can do here now," Charlie said. "They won't transfer the goods until tomorrow night. We'll plan to explore the mansion Saturday and look for the secret room."

"Oh, how cool!" Nancy smiled.

Rae's camera flicked.

"Look at that flash!" Nate yelled. "Somebody's over there. Let's get 'em!" Nate and the two men lunged toward them.

"Push the boxes over," Charlie told his friends.

Nate and the men yelled as the boxes tumbled onto them.

"Run! Get out!" Rick shouted.

Suddenly, Charlie tripped over a fallen box. His heart pounded as he struggled to get on his feet. His body felt rigid and his mouth speechless. Finally, he stood, calling out. "Hurry! Take the shortcut through the woods. Those guys are getting closer. And boy, do they look mad!"

Before they reached the woods, Nancy stumbled. "Ow! My wrist."

The friends slowed down to help her. Charlie looked around in desperation. He saw a large, muddy, swampy area beside them. He called to Rae. "Stay with Nancy. Rick, follow me."

Before he knew it, a voice blared, "Now we've got you!"

Charlie stood frozen, his stomach twisting into a knot. He could only stare at Nate and the men.

Rick turned toward them. "Look out! There's a snake behind you!" he shouted with a trembling voice.

Rick's warning startled them. They bumped into each other, becoming entangled. "Watch what you're doing!" Nate yelled at the men.

Rick said, "Push them in the swamp." He and Charlie rushed at the tangled bunch and with mighty shoves pushed them into the wet spongy slime.

Nate's head bobbed up and down. "You creeps just wait. We'll get you!"

Nancy held her arm close to her body. She and Rae ran over to the boys. "I think we got *you* this time, Nate," Rae yelled.

"Run!" Rick called. "This way!"

Rae grabbed Nancy's good arm, and the sleuths disappeared into the woods, leaving the threesome struggling in the mud.

"Man, what a close escape!" Charlie wiped his sweaty palms on his jeans. "I was scared stiff and didn't know what to do. Good thinking, Rick."

"Yeah, Rick, you were like a hero in the movies." Nancy tested her wrist, wincing.

Rick patted Charlie on the back. "Everything's okay now."

"You're right." He took a deep breath. "Now we need to be serious. We learned a lot of information in that warehouse. We've got to go to the police."

"Suppose they catch the robbers tonight and put it in the newspaper?" Nancy asked.

"Won't that blow our plan to catch the school 'phantoms'?" Rae asked.

"Maybe," Charlie answered. "I know my grandpa's best friend, Chief Howard, will understand and work with us. We need a few more days to complete our investigation. We've got to find the secret room and get proof of the stolen items at the mansion."

"You've got it," Rick agreed as they headed to the police station.

God, thank you for taking care of my friends and me. We might have gotten hurt or in a lot of trouble. Why does Nate want to hang out with those people?

As the friends walked through the door of the police station, Chief Howard motioned for them to come into his office. Charlie reported all the information they heard at the warehouse, and what happened there.

"Thanks for the tip about the hit at the museum and jewelry store," Chief Howard said. "But Charlie, you kids need to be really careful. These guys are dangerous! We'll work with you and let you finish your investigation. Let me know every move you make."

"Yes, sir," Charlie replied. "We'll need to explore the Mason Mansion for the secret room and proof of the stolen items. Will Saturday be okay?"

"I'll agree under one condition. Take this cell phone. Call me if there's any trouble. Just press and hold the seven. It'll automatically dial my cell phone."

"You got it, Chief." Charlie shook his hand. "Oh, please keep any word about capturing the crooks out of the news. We don't want to blow our plan to catch the school thieves in the act."

"Sure, I can keep it quiet," Chief Howard agreed.

Chapter 10
THE SECRET ROOM

At their lockers, Charlie showed Nancy a newspaper article. "See, I told you Chief Howard wouldn't let us down. By the way, how's your wrist today?"

"Oh, much better." They looked up to see Rick and Rae, hurrying to join them.

"Did you read in *The Pinesdale Gazette* about the robberies at Jenkins' Jewelry and the Martin Museum?" Charlie asked. "The newspaper didn't mention the capture of any thieves. Chief Howard kept his word. He called me early this morning to say he had two suspects locked up in his jail. Now, we need to find the secret room!"

"Hey, y'all." Rae swung her book bag. "I've got some important evidence to show you. Remember when I took pictures at the museum and warehouse? Well, last night my dad helped me print them. You'll never believe these!" She beamed, holding up two glossy pictures.

"There's Nate in the museum!" Nancy exclaimed.

Rick pointed to the other picture. "And there he is with those two guys at the warehouse."

"Guess my camera came in handy after all, even if it did make some noise and a flash." Rae grinned. "Will this help with the proof we need?"

"You bet it will," Charlie answered.

Nancy, did you ask your mom about spending the weekend with me?" Rae put her arm around her new friend.

"Sure, she was glad because my Aunt Trudy is sick in Ashview. My mom needs to go see about her."

"We'll have a great time," Rae said.

"It'll be totally awesome!" Nancy giggled.

"Oh, man—girls!" Rick poked Charlie.

"We need to meet at my house early in the morning. Then, we'll go search the mansion for the secret room. Everybody ready for that?"

"It's creepier each time I go, but it won't be too bad." Rae linked her arm in Nancy's. "At least we'll all be together."

Early Saturday morning, the sleuths hurried to the old mansion.

Nancy stepped inside. "Glad it's not dark."

Charlie led the way. "Let's explore the ballroom. The legend told about people hearing beautiful music coming from there." White sheets covered the piano and some chairs. A chandelier with missing crystals hung from the ceiling. *Bang!* A cracked mirror fell to the floor, inches from Charlie. "Wow! That was close!"

Creeeak!

"W-what's that?" Nancy stammered as she took a step back, bumping into Rae and Rick.

The sleuths stood, petrified. There was the sound again: *Creeeak!* It almost sounded like a groan.

Carol A. Lanier

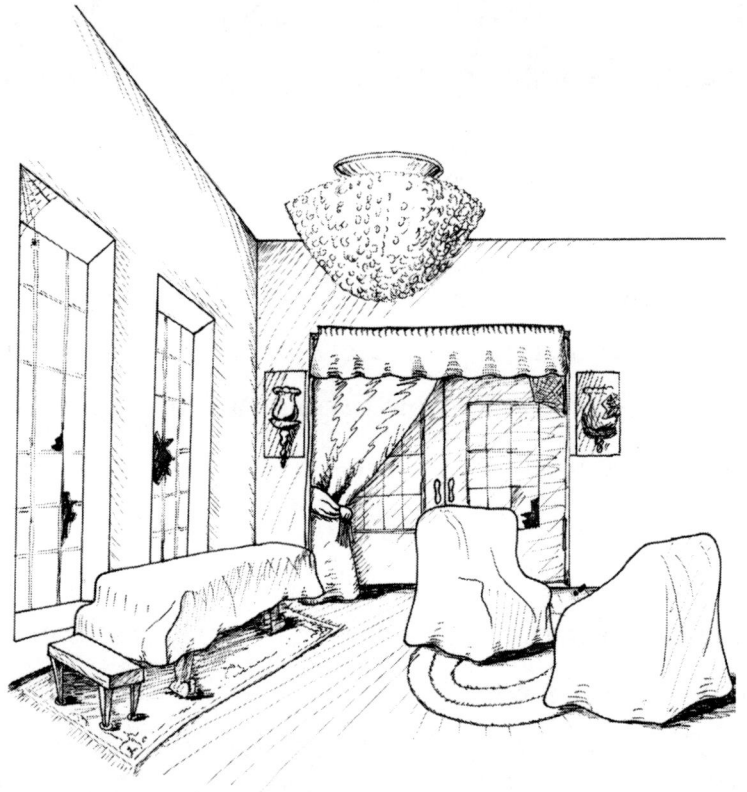

"Is it the old floors?" Rae whispered. "Or, maybe someone is in here."

Inching nearer to the creaking sound, Charlie heard faint voices and the rustling of papers. Rick peeked around the ballroom door into the entryway. There stood the strange man again— the one with gray hair, a beard, and a greenish tattoo. He was talking to a short, fat, bald guy.

Rick nudged Charlie. "That's one of the men from the warehouse."

"What was that noise, Joe?" the bearded man growled in a harsh voice.

"Probably one of those crooked mirrors fell. This old place is full of creaky noises, too. Let's go. We have things to do." The men headed out the front door.

"Come on," Charlie said. "We've got to find the secret room before they come back. We need to get our proof. Let's start over here."

"See this old fireplace," Rae said. "It's really dirty."

Charlie leaned over to look and accidentally fell against it. Without his noticing, the chief's cell phone slipped out of his pocket and landed in the far corner of the blackened fireplace. He grabbed the mantel to catch his balance. *Whoosh!* A panel next to it opened. Charlie grasped Rae's and Nancy's hands, pulling them into a room. "Come on, Rick."

The panel slid closed, leaving them in total darkness. It felt damp and smelled musty. Charlie pulled out a pocket flashlight, and the dim light shone on a rough floor.

Nancy clutched Rae's hand. "Where are we?"

"Maybe the secret room," Charlie warned. "Shhh! I hear something moving over there."

"Can you see anything?" Rick asked.

"No, this light isn't very bright." The flashlight went out. "Oh, no," Charlie grumbled, giving it a shake. "I forgot to check the batteries. Let's find what's making the noise."

On hands and knees, the sleuths crawled forward on the cold floor, feeling their way toward the sound. They moved slowly, scared of what they might find.

As they crept along, something scampered across Rae's hand. "Eeeeek! What was that thing?" she screamed.

"Don't be so loud," Rick whispered. "Probably just a little mouse, more afraid of you than you are of it. Now, shhh! Somebody might hear us."

"This place is creepy," Rae said. "Let's walk instead of crawl. There are too many gross things on the floor."

Inside the hidden room, the sleuths stumbled their way in the darkness.

"It's sure dark in here," Nancy complained. "How will we ever get out?"

"Hey, I hear a noise," Rick said. "You think it's those men?"

Charlie paused to listen. "Shhh! I hear a door opening. Hide!"

"But where?" Rae asked. "It's so dark."

"I feel a desk or something over here," Rick answered. "Hurry! Get behind it." A flash of light swept past them. They sat in silent panic. Charlie reached into his pocket for the cell phone. *It's not here! How did I lose it? Where is it?*

"Let's get this out and ready to load up," a rough voice said.

After a short while, Charlie heard only silence. "Y'all, I've got some bad news. I can't find the cell phone. Looks like we are on our own. We've got to get out of here before they come back and find us!"

In desperation, Charlie groped the wall for a way out. Finally, his head bumped an odd metal object that swung away from him like a pendulum. "Wait, I think I found something." He felt around, discovering what seemed to be a knob. Twisting it to the right, a flickering light began to beam. "It's a lantern, probably left here by the thieves. This is definitely the Mason Mansion secret room!"

Sticky cobwebs drooped from the ceiling and corners. The friends huddled together, trying to figure a way out. Nancy pointed to the floor. "What's this gold sparkling thing?"

"It might be from the stolen coin collection," Charlie said. "Let me see it, Nancy. It *is* a stolen coin! And look here. Is this drugs?" He held up a small plastic bag. "It has white powdery stuff in it!"

"Oh, wow! You're right," Rick agreed. "The thieves sure missed it."

Charlie wrapped the coin and bag in his handkerchief and put it in his pocket. "Think, everybody. There's got to be a way out of here." He closed his eyes, trying to picture where a door might be. The lantern tilted back and forth, and hit against something next to him.

"Hey, what's that noise?" Rae asked. She looked twice before seeing a small wooden chest covered with dust. "Rick, help me open this."

He fiddled with the tight clasp until it popped open. "Whoa! Will you look at this? A chest full of silverware! The thieves must have been in a real hurry to leave something so valuable."

"It looks like the chest in the picture you found in the dining room," Nancy said.

Rae remembered the one they found earlier. "Sure, the mother and the daughter."

"Do you think we have enough proof now, Charlie?" Nancy asked.

"Oh, yeah. A gold coin, a silver chest, and powdery stuff that might be drugs. I would say so!"

"And my pictures," Rae piped up.

"Yeah, your pictures," Charlie said. "Right now, we need to find a way out."

Chapter 11
TRAPPED!

"Looks as if we've come to a dead end," Charlie grumbled. "Thought we found the way out, but guess we didn't. I think we're in trouble!"

"Oh, no!" Nancy groaned. "I don't want to stay here. It's too scary."

The room does feel eerie. Something isn't right. "These robbers have a smooth operation. Now I know why Nate wanted us to think the mansion was haunted. My theory *is* right. Nate's one of the 'phantoms'."

"Well, he didn't want us to find the secret room, that's for sure," Rick said.

"Or the stolen items," Nancy added.

"What'll we do now?" Rae asked.

"We aren't quitters," Charlie answered. "We'll keep looking for a way out. At least we have a light. Let's keep going."

God, please help us escape. Charlie slid his shaking hand along the wall. Holding up the lantern, his eyes tried to focus. Finally, he caught sight of a strange object. He turned a hook-shaped handle, and a door flew open! He stepped into the kitchen.

"Way to go, Charlie!" Rick slapped him on the back.

When Charlie turned to leave, he saw a stairway leading to the second floor. "I'm curious to see where this goes. How about the rest of you?"

"I don't know," Rick replied. "It was scary in the secret room."

"I thought we'd never get out," Rae added.

"Bet this was the stairs for the servants," Nancy said. "I've read a lot about old houses."

"Come on. Let's check it out," Charlie suggested.

"Maybe there's an attic with some hidden treasures!" Rae smiled.

"Sure hope we won't get in trouble up there," Nancy said.

They began climbing the creaking staircase, trying to make as little noise as possible. The steps brought them to a landing on the second floor. The long hallway had several doors on either side. Opening the first one on his right, Charlie peered inside to find a large room, empty except for an ornate fireplace. "These bedrooms must have been for the family and their guests."

"Boy, there sure are a lot of bedrooms in this place." Rick counted. "My house only has three. There're twelve rooms off this hall."

"Come on. Let's go up the next flight of stairs." Charlie started ahead. The second flight led into another hallway with doors. Looking into a few, he found the rooms smaller and without fireplaces.

"Who stayed in these rooms?" Rae asked.

"I think they were for the servants."

Halfway down the hall, Charlie saw Nancy looking up into an opening. "What do you see?" he asked, coming to stand beside her. Another set of steps, very narrow and steep, led to a closed door. "Where does that go?"

"I'm guessing it leads to an attic. My grandmother lives in an old house, and she has steps like these to her attic."

"Oh, wow! I know we'll find some treasures up there. Let's go!" Rae clutched the knob but groaned. "Oh, no. It's locked! We'll never get to explore the attic."

"Wait a minute," Charlie said in a calm voice. "Look to your right."

"I don't see a thing."

"Look up higher."

Craning her head back, Rae finally saw a large key hanging on a big rusty nail. "Bet this is the key," she said.

"Probably. Can you reach it?" Charlie pointed from two steps behind her.

Standing on the top step, Rae stretched on her tiptoes and lifted the key off the nail. "Here, Charlie, you open it."

He squeezed past Nancy and put the key into the keyhole. He heard a raspy sound as he twisted it. The door swung open. The friends stood close

Charlie Hooper, Detective:

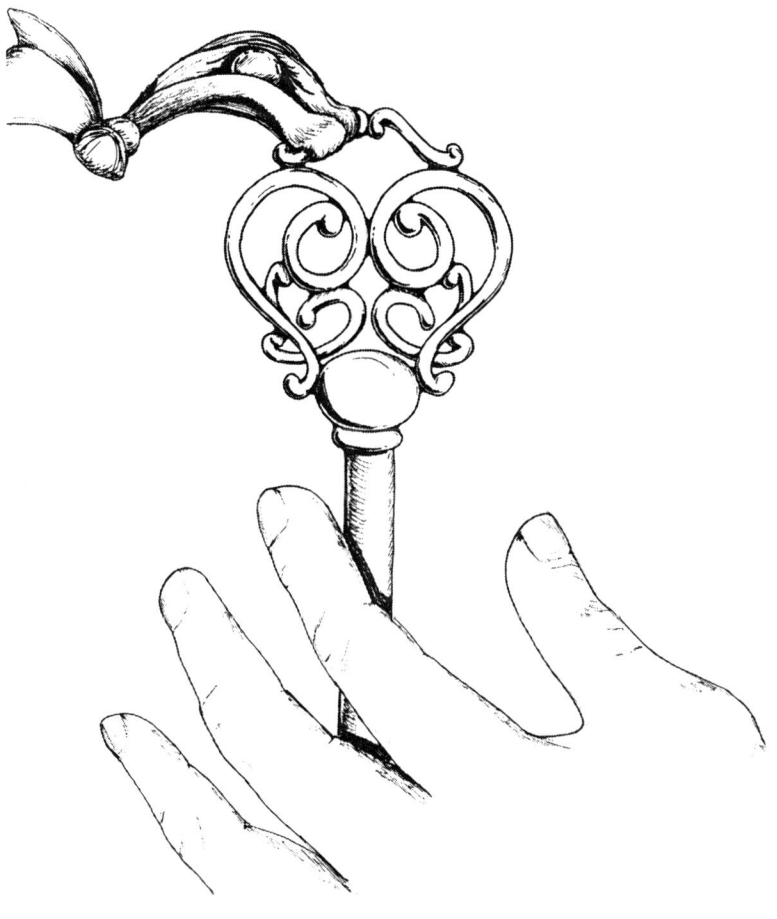

together inside the doorway. In the huge space they saw trunks, frames and other old things.

Rae looked around at the cluttered dusty room. In a far corner, she saw a unusual antique chest with drawers of different sizes. She ran to it and pulled at an odd-sized top drawer. "Hey, guys! Help me with this. It's stuck." She gave another strong tug. It flew open. "Never mind, I got it."

Nancy reached her hand into the drawer and pulled out a pearl-covered jewelry case. "Whoa, I've never seen anything so beautiful!" The sleuths' eyes widened.

"Hurry!" Charlie urged. "Open it so we can see what's inside."

Nancy opened the jeweled case. Inside, there was a sparkling emerald necklace, a matching pin and a ring with an emerald stone.

"Who do they belong to?" Rae asked. "They must've belonged to the owner of Mason Mansion long ago."

"Wait." Charlie reached inside the drawer. "I feel something else way in the back." He touched the object, then gripped it with his hand and took it out. "This looks like a diary."

The sleuths sat on an old bench. Charlie began to read. *"This diary belongs to Corinna Lacy Mason."* Charlie skipped some pages. "Here's one entry:

"*Monday, February 14, 1863.*

"*I am anxiously awaiting the arrival of James Colton, my first love. We plan to marry in the spring of this year. It is Valentine's Day, a day of romance and love. He promised to bring me a special surprise. I hear the doorbell ringing. He is here.*

"The next entry is February 15, 1863.

"*James brought me the most wonderful gift I have ever received! It is a lovely pearl jewelry case with a sparkling emerald necklace, matching brooch and ring, all belonging to his late grandmother. He told me he is giving me these treasures to deeply convey his love, and that I was to wear them on our wedding day. How joyful and full of love I feel in my heart!*

"*Friday, February 18, 1863:*

"James informed me today he will be leaving for the war next week. We will have to postpone our wedding until his return.

"The last entry recorded is May 18, 1863.

"I have been patiently waiting for my love's return. I have not heard from him in three months. I will hide my precious gems upstairs in the attic until his welcomed return."

"My grandmother told me Miss Mason learned about her fiancé's death in the war and she never married," Charlie said.

"How sad," Rae said. "The man she planned to marry never returned."

"It's strange no one has found this until now," Rick said. "What are we going to do with it?"

"We'll take it to the police and let them decide. This mansion has a lot of history. Bet they'll put it in the historical museum with other Civil War items," Charlie said. He handed the case and diary to Rae. "Here, put this in your backpack for safe keeping."

Rae patted the bag. "Sure, I'll take good care of it."

"Let's hurry and get this evidence to the police," Charlie urged. He started down the steps and the others followed. Nearing the bottom of the staircase that led into the kitchen, Charlie stopped and whispered, "Be quiet. I hear something." He hesitated, looking around cautiously.

They huddled at the bottom of the stairs, straining to hear. Two men stepped in front of them. The one with the tattoo pointed a gun right at Charlie. "What are ya kids doing here, and what's in the bag?" he demanded.

Charlie's eyes grew wide with fright. "We-ee-ee like exploring old houses." His voice cracked. "Aa-a-and, this is some of our snacks."

The grouchy man grabbed the bag from Rae and peered inside. "Snacks, huh? I'll keep this pretty thing. Don't you know snoopin' can get you in trouble?"

Rae took a step back in panic. Nancy grabbed her arm and Rick stared in fear. The man poked the gun in Charlie's ribs and nudged him to move forward. "Joe, look what I found." He showed his partner the pearl-encrusted box.

The short pudgy guy paced the floor. "You ain't really gonna shoot 'em, are you, Mack?"

"Oh, hush. Take 'em to the cellar. Tie their hands and feet, and gag 'em."

"B-But...where are you going?"

"I'm leaving to check on business." Mack scowled. "Hurry up. Meet me at the warehouse when you're done."

Joe forced them down the cellar steps into the dark basement, lit only by two windows near ceiling level.

Squeak! Squeak!

"Don't put us down here," Nancy cried. "That sounds like mice!"

Charlie's heart pounded. He accidentally bumped into a box, knocking it over. *Crash!* It tumbled to the floor. *God, I'm really scared. Show me what to do.*

"Wh-what's that?" Joe stammered nervously.

"Maybe a 'ghost'." Rick bumped against him, causing his gun to fall by Rae's foot. She hurriedly kicked it across the room.

"Now look what you did. Sit down and hush, you little twerps," Joe growled. He lumbered into the basement's shadows, where he fumbled for his gun.

Charlie saw his chance to get away. He quickly headed out of the cellar, stepping on the outside of each step to avoid creaking too much.

"Here's my gun." Joe stuck it inside the waist of his pants. He was clumsy in the dim light as he taped their wrist, ankles and mouths. "You kids better be still and quiet. Mack's really mean. I'm goin' to go meet 'im."

Joe tramped up the cellar steps, slamming the door at the top. The three friends looked at each other, amazed Joe hadn't noticed there were only three kids instead of four!

Charlie looked around the kitchen with caution, and then headed to the back door. He twisted the knob, breathing a sigh of relief when it opened onto a porch. He hurried down the three steps and squatted low, looking around.

To his right, he saw the outdoor steps leading down to the basement door. Moving there, he noticed the area at the bottom of the stairs covered with a thick layer of dry leaves. Charlie walked as quietly as possible to the door. It was locked!

How can I get back in the cellar without going inside the mansion? I'll hide here for five minutes in case Joe comes this way. His watch seemed to take way longer than five minutes, but finally he felt it was safe to try the windows for a way in.

Hurrying back up the steps, he crouched low behind some cedar bushes and checked the window. It was shut tightly. He could see his friends sitting patiently on the dirt floor. Rick raised his bound hands and gave him a thumbs-up. Crab-walking to the next window, Charlie checked it to see if it was loose. He pushed it open enough to squirm through, landing inside the cellar with a thump.

"Mmmm!" Rick raised his eyebrows. Charlie pulled the tape off Rick's mouth and then the girls'. "Boy! Am I glad to see you. Get us untied. You have your pocketknife, don't you? Good work. You're one sneaky dude!"

Rae rubbed her wrists. "I'm glad to be free of that sticky duct tape?"

"This has certainly been another adventure." Nancy sighed. "It's a good thing Joe isn't real smart. Thanks, Charlie."

"We know who the ringleaders are in this operation," Charlie explained. "Now, we can give the police accurate descriptions and first names. Remember when I told you about that strange man hanging around the school? I knew I had seen him somewhere. It was Mack! And don't forget what we found in the secret room!" He patted his pocket.

"We'll have to tell the police about the silver chest, since we left it here in the mansion," Rae said.

"I'm ready to get out of this place!" Nancy walked to the bottom of the cellar steps. "Hurry! What if Joe or Mack decide to come back?"

"Okay, let's go. We can talk on the way to police headquarters," Charlie said. "It's important to turn this new evidence in. The next thing we've got to do is catch the school thieves in the act!"

Chapter 12

TROUBLE AT THE GAZEBO

Charlie and the sleuths burst into the police station. "Is Chief Howard here?" Charlie asked. "It's important that I see him."

"No," the desk sergeant said. "He and most of the detectives are out on a new case. A bank robbery occurred early this morning. I'm Sergeant Langford. Would you like to leave a message?"

"Yes, my name is Charlie Hooper and we're The Pinesdale Sleuths. Chief Howard knows all about the case we're working on. We have some great new evidence for him. Be sure to keep it safe. I'll give him all the details later."

Charlie pulled out his handkerchief with the gold coin and the bag of white powdery stuff and handed it to the sergeant. "Thanks. Oh, and tell Chief Howard we'll be at the Mason Mansion."

"I'll lock this up in the evidence room and tell the chief as soon as he gets back. Good work. You kids be careful."

"Do you think the thieves will go back for the silver chest?" Nancy asked as they walked out of the building.

"You betcha," Charlie answered. "That's why we have to go back into the mansion for it. We need all the evidence we can get to solve this case." He looked at his friends. "What do you think? Are you up to it?"

"I'm not really excited about going back there, but let's get it over with," Nancy said.

"I've got a large backpack and a good flashlight at my house," Rick said, as they headed toward Charlie's. "We can swing by there and pick them up."

"Great." Charlie nodded. "We'll go by my house and get a snack. Meet us in my front yard in a few minutes."

"Got it!" Rick called, slamming his front door as he ran to meet his friends. "Let's get going. It's only a couple of hours 'til dark." The friends hopped on their bikes and pedaled along, munching on granola bars.

The sleuths approached the mansion with caution. "We've got to be careful," Charlie said. "We can't get caught this time."

They crept into the mansion, heading to the ballroom. "I'll try pushing against the mantel again. Do you have the flashlight, Rick?"

"You bet I do, and it's a big one! I put new batteries in it, too."

"That's good, Rick, but don't rub it in just because I forgot to check the batteries last time."

Charlie leaned against the fireplace and, as eerily as before, the panel slid open. "Hurry! Let's get in before it closes. Rick, you go in first with the light." They hurried into the room.

Charlie couldn't believe his eyes. There, in the far corner of the fireplace, was Chief Howard's cell phone. The panel closed, leaving him in the ballroom. "So, that's where it landed. It fell out of my pocket when I stumbled. Thank you, Lord, for letting me find it." He scooped up the phone and pressed against the mantel again. The panel swooshed open and Charlie stepped into the secret room. As soon as he was in, the panel closed.

"What happened to you?" Rick asked.

Nancy grabbed his arm and gave it a shake. "You scared us to death!"

"Yeah, what's goin' on?" Rae demanded.

"Sorry to scare you, but look what I found." He held up the cell phone. "I saw it in the fireplace just as the panel was closing. I had to get it. Come on, let's get done with what we need to do."

"Wow, it's still pretty dark, even with our flashlight," Nancy said.

"Yeah, and as spooky as ever." Rae shuddered. "I hope that gross mouse isn't still here."

"We've got to find the chest and get out," Rick said. "Charlie, you take the light and lead the way."

He guided his friends along the wall and shined the light all around to catch a glimpse of the chest. After looking in every nook and cranny, Charlie plopped down and leaned against the wall. "The chest isn't here. One of the thieves must've come back for it. Now what?"

"Where would they have taken it?" Nancy asked.

"If it's not here, it's got to be at the warehouse, the boathouse, or the gazebo, right?" Rae asked.

"Let's think where the logical place would be," Rick said. "The chest isn't that big."

"I don't think they would take it to the warehouse yet. They probably took it to the gazebo first. Then, they'll move it and the other goods to the warehouse. From there, they'll take it out of town to sell and get money for drugs." Charlie motioned. "I think I remember the way to the kitchen door. Follow me."

In a few minutes, the sleuths stood in the kitchen. They hurried out of the mansion to their bikes. Their tires dug in the dirt, leaving dust hanging in the air.

They parked their bikes in the tall weeds near the gazebo, like before. "Is anybody around?" Nancy asked.

"It doesn't look like it," Charlie said. "Rae, hand me the bag."

"Here, it's ready to load."

"The rest of you stay down. Rick, give a whistle if there's trouble."

He took one look around the tall bush before stepping out toward the gazebo. No one was in sight. Running as fast as he could, Charlie reached the steps and knelt low. He looked into the gazebo. His eyes grew big with amazement. There was the silver chest, along with the pearl-jeweled case, some stacked boxes, a small TV, and a DVD player. "Hey, get a load of all this loot!"

"Why would they go off and leave it unguarded?" Rae asked.

"It might mean they're coming back any minute," Charlie answered. "Hurry and put the silver chest in the bag. Nancy put the jewelry case in the basket of your bike. We've got to get out of here!"

"Hold it, I think I hear their SUV!" Rick said. "We better stay hidden until they leave."

"At least we have some more evidence," Nancy said.

Charlie Hooper, Detective:

After hiding behind the bushes, Charlie whispered, "Stay low and quiet."

"There's Lefty and Nate," Nancy whispered back.

"What's this?" Lefty asked. "Some of our loot is gone. Do you know anything about this, Nate? Have your friends been pokin' around again?".

"They're not my friends. I don't know what happened to the stuff."

"Maybe whoever took it is still around," Lefty said. "Start lookin' for 'em. I'll go this way. You look here."

Ah-chooo! Rae let out a sneeze.

"Shhh." Charlie poked her.

The weeds parted. There stood Nate, glaring at them. "So it *is* you! Hey, Lefty, over here."

Rae stood and kicked him in the shin. "Ow!" Nate bent over and grabbed his leg.

Quickly, Charlie lifted the heavy bag and banged Nate on the head. "Hurry! Get out of here!"

They jumped on their bikes and pedaled as fast as they could.

"Fine work, detectives," Chief Howard said. "Sergeant Langford showed me the evidence you brought in earlier. Charlie, you're getting to be as good a detective as your grandfather. He'd be so proud. Now, all of you sit down and tell me how you got this great evidence."

Once settled in chairs, Charlie reached into his pocket and took out the cell phone. "Thanks for loaning this to me, sir."

"You're welcome. I'm glad you didn't have to use it."

"Well, uh, actually we did need to, but, uh…"

"What are you trying to say, Charlie?"

"Well, sir, the phone fell out of my pocket before we went into the secret room. But, I didn't know it. When we thought we were in trouble, it was missing. God really protected us."

"Yes, He did." Chief Howard took the phone. "You kids took a great risk. You could have been seriously hurt or even killed. Those crooks are really bad. But tell me, how did you get the phone back if you lost it?"

Carol A. Lanier

Charlie and his friends spent a long time that afternoon with Chief Howard, telling him about everything.

Chapter 13

THE HIDDEN CABIN

Rain poured, lightning flashed, and thunder crashed at dawn on Sunday morning. Charlie awoke to wailing sirens zooming down Mason Avenue, just at the end of his street. After dressing, he scampered down the stairs with his shirt unbuttoned. He heard the radio reporter announce a fire at the Mason Mansion. "Mom, can I go?"

"I guess so. Stay out of the way and be careful."

He slung his backpack over his shoulder and ran for the door.

"Button your shirt," his mom called to him.

By the time The Pinesdale Sleuths arrived at the scene, the storm had cleared and a rose-colored sky peeked through the clouds. Wet grass glistened as flames blazed from the windows and roof. Charlie felt the heat of the fire washing over him. Police cars, fire trucks and ambulances were parked all around.

"What a mess!" Charlie choked.

"It's awful," Rae said with tears in her eyes. "Thank goodness the police have already investigated the secret room."

"Lightning started the fire," Rick said. "I overheard the fire chief tell a reporter."

Right then, they heard a loud crash as the center of the mansion's burning roof collapsed. "Oh, no!" Charlie put his hand to his forehead. "What else is going to happen?"

Out of the corner of his eye, he spotted a flash in the darkness of the woods. He began scanning the grounds of the estate to the right of the mansion. "What was that? A light? Let's go."

They skirted the fire trucks clustered in front of the mansion. The sleuths found a narrow winding path at the edge of the woods. Branches of pine trees dipped down low, slapping raindrops against them as they inched farther into the wooded area. Their shoes squished in the wet with each step they took. The weather felt hot and muggy even in the shade of the trees. Twigs, pine straw and cones covered the ground from the storm.

"Watch out!" Nancy yelled, leaping over some poison ivy. A brown lizard scurried across her feet and zipped up the trunk of an oak tree. "Ooo! I don't like lizards!"

The rippling blue lake sparkled off to their left. Charlie heard the sputtering of an engine, and then a steady chugging. He looked across the lake to see a motorboat speeding across to the pier near the old gazebo.

Nancy pointed down another rough trail toward the lake. "Look. An old bridge."

Covered with chipped paint, a bridge sagged over a small stream. Several boards were loose. It swayed as if someone had walked across it moments before.

Charlie looked beyond the bridge. "It looks like the trail leads to the pier and boathouse at the edge of the lake."

"Why is that boat speeding across?" Rae asked.

"Maybe to smuggle out more stolen goods or drugs," Charlie concluded. "That's probably why I saw the flash of light in the woods. Chief Howard told us he suspected drug involvement."

Rick shook his head. "They won't be able to use the mansion for storage or drug smuggling anymore."

"You're right. The secret room's gone," Nancy said. "They only have the warehouse for storage now."

"Why're they operating during the day?" Rae asked. "Aren't they afraid someone will see them?"

"There's so much confusion and commotion at the mansion this morning, they think no one'll notice them," Charlie said.

"Let's go back to the main trail and see where it leads," Rick suggested.

After a short way, they stopped. There stood a rustic old cabin with honeysuckle vines entwined all around. The coarse vines crisscrossed the dirty windowpanes, and Spanish moss hung from oak branches. A willow tree drooped over the eaves of the front door.

Charlie jumped over a large tree branch that had fallen during the storm. "This cabin looks old." Without hesitation, he entered it. The others followed.

"Man," Rick whispered, staring at a wrinkled-up blanket on a cot in the corner. "Looks like somebody lives here."

"Anyone for coffee?" Rae called in a teasing voice. "The pot's still warm."

"Somebody must love Georgia peaches as much as I do," Nancy said. "Look at those pits left on the table."

"Someone's been here, that's for sure," Charlie agreed.

"Maybe they were going to build a fire." Rae pointed to a pile of wood on the hearth of the stone fireplace.

Whoosh! A bat flew out from the rafters past Rae. "Get it out of here!" she screamed.

"Yeah!" Nancy shouted. "It's disgusting!"

Charlie grabbed a broom, striking the bat and scaring it out the cabin door. Putting the broom back, he noticed something on the wide plank floor. "What's this?" he asked, picking up a ring, its gem sparkling like a star.

"It looks like a red ruby ring!" Rae reached to take it from him. "It's a valuable jewel, one of the most precious on earth. I read about it in the book called *Gemstones of the World*. Here, Charlie, put this in your pocket to keep it safe."

"Sure thing! This is evidence for the police!"

"Do you think a robber brought the jewelry here yesterday before taking it to the secret room?" Nancy asked.

They heard the swishing of leaves outside the cabin. A face peered through the window at them. "Look!" Rick yelled. "One of the robbers!"

"He must have come back to search for the missing ring!" Charlie shouted. "After him!"

Chapter 14
THE CHASE

The sleuths hustled out of the cabin as the man disappeared into the sweeping shadows of the woods.

Rae tripped over a tree root and sprawled onto the pine straw. "Ooh!" she cried as she held her bleeding knee.

Nancy knelt down to help her. "I'll stay with Rae. We'll catch up later. Follow that man!"

Charlie and Rick raced after the robber, dodging the low, wet, hanging branches, but still getting smacked in the face. The man stopped suddenly, noticing the police and fire trucks beyond the edge of the thicket.

"Close in. Nab him," Charlie whispered. They tiptoed toward the man. *Thud!* A dead tree limb fell behind them. Charlie grabbed Rick.

The robber twirled around to face them. "You nosy little twerps," he snarled. "Now you'll get it!"

The man picked up a fallen branch and broke it over Rick's head. Rick fell and lay still. Shaking like a leaf, Charlie threw up his arms to protect his head. The man curled his fist and punched him in the face, knocking him to the ground. He reached down, slipped a note into Charlie's pocket, and then headed toward the lake.

When the boys came to, they slowly sat up. "Oh-hhh, my head feels like a spinning top." Rick moaned. "What happened?"

"The robber knocked us out and got away. Why haven't Rae and Nancy shown up yet? I hope they're not lost." Looking up, Charlie saw the girls approaching. "Thank goodness," he murmured as he and Rick started to stand.

"You boys look awful!" Rae limped through the vines, looking surprised.

"Watch out!" Charlie hollered, seeing a copperhead snake crawling out from under a wisteria bush. It arched its body. The girls' eyes popped out with fear as they stood behind the snake. The reptile struck Rick, clamping its fangs into his ankle. Then the snake slithered away. Rick's ankle dripped with blood.

"Boy, does that sting!" Rick yelled and bit his lip, tears streaming down his cheeks.

"What'll we do now?" Rae cried. "His ankle is swelling and turning red."

Charlie started taking off his belt. "I took a first aid class in P.E. I know what to do. Give me Rick's belt. Are you ready?"

Rick nodded, holding Rae's hand with a firm grip. He closed his eyes, tensing his leg. Charlie fastened the belts above Rick's ankle. Then he sucked the venom from the bite and spat it out.

The girls covered their eyes and squealed, "Ewwwww!"

Ignoring them, he did it several more times. Finally, he pulled his water bottle from his backpack and rinsed his mouth. Feeling exhausted from the chaotic morning, Charlie wrapped Rick's ankle with his handkerchief. "We'd better get going! We need to get help quick."

"Which way? I'm all turned around." Nancy shook with uneasiness in her voice and panic in her eyes. "I can't see. There's not much light under these trees."

"Don't worry, I know the way." Charlie threw Rick's arm around his shoulder and put his arm around Rick's waist. "Rae, you and Nancy steady him on the other side."

The friends struggled forward, slinging branches from their faces. They headed toward the edge of the thicket to the winding path leading to the mansion. When they stepped out of the trees, Charlie waved to a nearby policeman. "Hey, we need help over here!"

The policeman took one look at the group and keyed his radio. "Paramedic needed at east side of property."

Soon, a paramedic rushed to their aid. Rick was transported to the hospital.

The police officer shook Charlie's hand. "Great job, kid. Your friend could have died without your quick thinking."

"Thank you, sir." Charlie slipped his hands into his pants pockets. "Wait a minute. We have something important to give to you." In his hand lay the ruby ring.

On their way home, Charlie reached into his shirt pocket. Pulling out some gum, a crumpled piece of paper fell out. "What's this? Not another note! How did it get here?" Smoothing it out, he looked flabbergasted.

Nancy looked over his shoulder. "What does it say?"

"'Warning! Meet me at the cabin at 1:00 p.m. or someone will get hurt!'" Charlie looked up. "It's signed, 'Nate'."

"You aren't going!" Rae insisted. "It might be a trap and Rick's not here to help."

"Well, I'm curious to see what he wants. I can't figure out how this note got into my pocket."

"Did you say you and Rick were knocked out by that robber you chased?" Nancy asked.

"You're right. We both have bumps that are humdingers!" Charlie gingerly touched his eyebrow.

Nancy peered at Charlie's face. "Wow. You even have a black eye!"

"Maybe the robber slipped the note into your pocket then," Rae suggested.

"Are you really going?" Nancy looked worried.

"Nate's not tricking me, I'll trick him. I'll notify the police. If I don't come out of the thicket in a few minutes, the police will come after me. Meanwhile, it'll be me against Nate."

The girls hooked their arms through his. "Be careful, Charlie!"

At 1:00, Charlie stood in position inside the cabin. He saw the cot, coffee pot, and wood by the hearth. He heard a footstep behind him and turned, ready to face Nate. Instead, he saw a sleazy man with a scar on his left cheek.

"See you showed up, kid," the shabby man said.

"Thought I was meeting Nate. Where is he?"

"Nate ain't comin'. My partner put that note in your pocket when you chased him from this cabin. Wha'd you do with the ring? Hand it over."

"What do you *think* I did with it? Give it to my girlfriend?" Charlie coughed nervously, hoping the police would show up any second.

"Being cute, eh?" The man grabbed Charlie by the arm and tried to pull him out the cabin door. Charlie clutched the doorjamb. "Let's take a little ride. Maybe your friends will come looking for you."

Charlie hung on and dug his heels into the ground, trying to stall for time. *God, where are the police?*

All of a sudden, Nate appeared behind the man! With his finger to his lips to silence Charlie, he crept close, knocking the man out with a rock. "Let's get out of here, Charlie. These guys play mean."

They walked away from the still form of the man. Charlie looked at him with surprise. "Why'd you help me, Nate? You're one of them."

"I didn't write that note. I heard some of them talking, so I knew something was up. I decided to follow the creepy guy. I don't really like them. I got all mixed up with the wrong crowd, and I don't know how to get out of it. Even though we've had our differences, I don't want you to get hurt, Charlie."

They heard the pounding of footsteps approaching. Charlie nodded. "That will be Chief Howard." Nate slipped away as quietly as he had appeared.

"Charlie, are you okay?" Chief Howard asked, out of breath. "You didn't come out in time."

"I'm fine, Chief. Your culprit is at the cabin."

Man, am I tired! This has been some day. I'm so glad Rick is okay. He punched his pillow and pulled the covers up to his chin.

God, Nate is hard to understand. He's angry with me, but he saved my life. Please help him to be safe. Show me a way to help him.

Chapter 15
COOKED CROOKS!

Before school on Monday morning, Charlie tapped his pencil on his notebook. "We need to discuss our plan. We have this case figured out. We know our theory is correct and we have our proof. However, we need to catch the 'phantoms' in the act. I've already reviewed our lists."

"Do you think they'll steal again?" Rick asked.

"Oh, yeah," Charlie said. "I don't think two times will give them enough cash. We've got to act fast and create a distraction and a trap. Are your walkie-talkies handy?"

"Roger that!" Rae answered.

Charlie stuffed his notebook and pencil into his backpack. "Let's go see Mrs. Pitts now."

"It sounds like a good plan, but I didn't realize we'd be dealing with such dangerous men," Mrs. Pitts said. "I better contact the police to be your backup. Then I'll notify Mr. Barton about the plan. We must make sure you kids are safe."

On the way to class, Rick caught sight of Nate. "Charlie, there's Nate by the lockers. Now's our chance."

Charlie gave him a thumbs-up. "Get movin'."

"Rick, did you hear about the new, expensive, compact microscope that arrived last week?" Charlie blared, hoping Nate would take the bait. "Can't wait to test it in science lab this afternoon."

"No, I didn't hear," Rick said. "Bet it's a beaut!" Nate's face lit up and he walked away.

At 1:30 that afternoon, Charlie sat in the science lab listening to Mr. Barton's instructions. He kept gazing at the door for Nate. With a low beep, his walkie-talkie came on. "Nate's on the way," Rae whispered from the girls' lookout station. After several minutes, Charlie noticed Nate approach the lab door. Nate stood, eyeing the microscope.

Come on in and take the bait. This has to work.

At 2:00 sharp, a fire drill sounded. *Rick's right on schedule with the plan!* In the confusion, Charlie hid inside the closet. He peeped out to watch Nate at the end of the line as the students filed out. In a second, Nate slipped back into the room and moved to the microscope. He pulled a cloth from his pocket and covered the instrument with it. Picking it up, he hurried out.

Following Nate, Charlie took a few steps, and then stopped. He heard something from behind, but no one seemed to be there. He took a deep breath to calm his racing heart. *I hope that sound is the police. I need some help, and where is Rick?* Then he heard voices coming from the gym.

"Hurry up, Nate!" Mr. Butler scolded. "What took so long?"

"Nothing. Made sure I wasn't followed."

"With everyone out of the building?" Mr. Butler reached out and grabbed the microscope. "Let's get this put away and get out of here before we're missed. We'll take it to the Mason Mansion cabin tonight."

Nate nodded. "Sure, Mr. Butler."

Charlie eased closer to the door. With knocking knees and trembling hands, he peered inside. *Clink!* His walkie-talkie slipped from his sweaty grip. Charlie stepped back.

Mr. Butler gave a startled jerk at the noise. He turned toward the door.

A hand gripped Charlie's shoulder. A voice whispered, "Charlie, it's me, Rick. The girls are here, too."

Mr. Butler clutched the microscope to his chest. "Do something, Nate!"

Nate charged. Charlie lunged forward, tackling him at the waist, slamming him to the floor. "Sorry, Nate," Charlie whispered in his ear.

"Freeze!" a voice ordered. "Alden Butler, you're under arrest for theft." An officer put handcuffs on Mr. Butler's wrists and led him away. "And you," he pointed to Nate, "come with me to the police station."

Charlie hesitated and then called, "Wait a minute! Can I speak to Nate?" He gently turned

Charlie Hooper, Detective:

Nate by the shoulders to face him. "I'm sorry for the mean things I said. I'll make sure Chief Howard knows how you helped me yesterday at the cabin. Maybe, when you get out of detention, we can work on being better friends. We can talk to other kids in school about not getting involved with drugs. There are some great programs we can use."

Nate smiled. "Would you really help me? Even after all I've done?"

"Of course, I will."

Nate smiled. "I'd like that. I want to do what's right."

"Sure, we'll be a team against drugs and crime."

Nate nodded as the officer led him out of the gym.

Charlie said, "You know, Nate might not be such a bad guy if he were around good adults and friends to teach him to do what's right."

"We'll all try to help him," Rae said.

"Cool!" Rick agreed.

"All right!" Charlie gave high-fives to his team. "About time! We did it. Another case solved. Race you to the treehouse!" He scrambled for a head start out of the gym.

"Hey, wait for us," Rick called.

Charlie lay his head on his pillow. *It feels great to lie down. Wow, what a day!* He thought about his grandpa and prayed. *God, thank you for teaching me to stick by a friend. Help me to always remember Proverbs 18:24: "... there is a friend who sticks closer than a brother." Thank you for giving me the courage to forgive Nate. And God, keep guiding me to be a great detective.*

A few weeks later, sitting in Charlie's treehouse, the sleuths discussed the news of Nate and Mr. Butler in the paper.

"We really nabbed those crooks," Charlie boasted.

"Did you see on the news last night about their arraignment?" Rick asked.

"I think Mr. Butler will be in prison for a long time," Rae said.

Charlie sat with his chin on his knees. "I hope Nate will get a light sentence and be out of detention in a few months."

Nancy pointed at the newspaper headline above their picture. "Look. 'Sharp-Witted Sleuths Help Solve Case!' I've never been famous before."

"I can't wait to see what our next case involves." Charlie jumped up and headed to the ladder. "But right now—I'm hungry! Let's see what my mom has to eat."

About the Author

Carol A. Lanier had no interest in writing, but God led her to do so. He continued tugging at her heart, until she decided to write for His honor.

A schoolteacher for thirty years, Carol gained much experience with her students, especially reluctant readers. Her desire is to develop a love of reading in all young people and to provide a Christian worldview through entertaining stories. She is a member of the Christian Writers Guild, the Georgia Writers Association, and the Heart of Georgia Writers Group.

She enjoys reading and hosting devotionals in her home in Warner Robins, Georgia. Her daughter and grandson reside in Atlanta.

CPSIA information can be obtained at www.ICGtesting.com
Printed in the USA
LVOW040349280712

291901LV00002B/5/P